T0146636

THE ENTITY PHYLUM

AUTHORS;
KEVIN J. STE. MARIE
& FRANCINE B.

authorHOUSE

AuthorHouse™
1663 Liberty Drive
Bloomington, IN 47403
www.authorhouse.com
Phone: 833-262-8899

Published by AuthorHouse 11/29/2023

ISBN: 978-1-5462-0340-7 (sc)
ISBN: 978-1-5462-0339-1 (hc)

Library of Congress Control Number: 2017912254

Print information available on the last page.

Contents

About The Characters

The Entity Phylum is a journey of the unknown for characters Plateeney & Agent Eph. The duo sign up for an unknown experience to better understand what they will encounter on future missions. The future missions start by interrogating 14 Entities that affect humans while on the planet Earth. They can receive this training after agreeing to no longer be a part of the human population. The characters are allowed to interrogate these unknown Entities mindlessly under the protection of others who have made the same leap as themselves. The knowledge learned as these interrogations occur has yet to be documented on Earth.

This knowledge can make others realize the human process has flaws in its programming, allowing these Entities to feed off their human hosts like parasites.

This knowledge is the proper understanding and experience one should receive before experiencing humanity.

Foreword

The energy that connects us to a soul to the vessel we exist in is God. The connection to our vessel to the output of the world is up to us.

What we choose to allow ourselves to believe and feel are our direct manifestations of what we know daily. If we choose to change, our vessel changes too. If we choose to stop, our soul disconnects and moves forward. If we choose to allow this world to take us over, we will not exist entirely of ourselves in our vessels on this planet. Just as our soul chooses a vessel as a host. An entity can also choose us as a vessel to ride on in time. We allow this to take place within us as a manipulation of our free will.

This is why it is so important to make sure that the things of this world are a part of God as well.

The most amazing gift ever created was a brain to allow us to electrify the vessels we choose to illuminate others with. When we choose to illuminate ourselves through negativity; an entity will attract and start his work on the slow disconnection of God to yourself; as well as the disconnection to the vessel to the soul. This lesson is the game of life, and the lesson always learned is that when you disconnect from God. You can never truly be yourself.

Entity 1

THE SEXUAL ENTITY

Ordinary humanity may not understand the world of 'the entities.' It is and has always been a secret. For some, we go about life just simply living. Understanding the world we 'see' or what our mind allows us to perceive is only one part of the 'puzzle.'

Agent Eph and Plateeney walk down the hallway of a room. This room does not exist in the ordinary reality that we see daily.

The room is a portal allowing access to dimensions, similar to a dream state. This state of awareness is only allowed by those who choose to allow changes in their consciousness. While here, Agent Eph & Plateeney are told they may cross-reference fourteen unique entities that somehow exist on the Earth. The regular human untrained eyes can not see these entities. A human must go through a 'process of elimination from the regular world they know. This process is called 'The Entity Phylum.' The entities reap many problems in many humans' lives today. This happens without humans having an awareness of knowing they exist.

Agent Eph & Plateeney may interview all entities individually.

{The following information concerns seven of the entity sources questioned. The interrogation team could cross-reference a human infested with three or more entities at the end of the interrogation. They approved this question to better understand what happens to many humans on Earth.}

{It is essential to understand that Agent Eph and Plateeney have chosen to see these entities' hidden dimensions for this level of questioning. The

1

information you are about to learn is unknown to the human psyche and has been since 1945. As the pair walk down these halls questioning these entities, you will learn what they sacrificed to learn for the first time. There are many questions and answers, but please be patient and understand the information is essential. The information is for humanity to process}

Agent Eph and Plateeney continue walking. The pair turns a corner to a large room with light yellow-colored walls.

As they approach, they notice one individual caged in a cubicle location. The figure looks like a woman leaning against an orange chair with curved armrests.

The Entity leaned back with a very egotistic nature. It had a visual of a woman. It arched her back as she moved from left to right like a provocative cobra in her chair. As she moved, like a cobra, she emitted negative energy in a spiral around the top of her aura like a small rust-colored tornado. The tornado created a strange barrier around her in some strange way.

This Entity looked around in circles, then explained slowly, "I don't care if I'm here. I can do what I want when I feel the need." This was a warning to the interrogators.

The Entity grew slightly tempered mentally. It seemed like this entity: 'The Sexual Entity' might try to stand at any minute. As she looked around, the air above her moved in circles. The Entity had a very dark attitude. You could almost feel it like an emitting frequency.

This Entity has the visual of a female but with very bizarre energy. The Entity didn't have a living presence within her, almost soulless by description. Something had visually flushed her face as if it drained the life force energy from her.

You could tell her blood flow was weak within her body. Her veins were visible with scratches & more prominent blue veins protruded through her delicate skin. It was like a vision of someone who had been stitched together. Identical to a tattered rag doll.

Someone loosely put together, still humanoid-looking, with very negative dark energy. When this entity made eye contact, you felt a slight pain in your chest. The sharp pain was like a paralysis attack, taking control of the body for a mere second, then regaining the ability to breathe again.

Apparently, after feeling the energy of this entity, one knows she does not play well with others. You would never know in the human consciousness because she cannot be seen with normal 'human' eyes. This is very important to remember.

Agent Eph and Plateeney realized that the room they were inside was not ordinary. But now, they processed the abnormal dimension and truly understood. The rust-colored tornado was also something only they could see in the room. Then, they realized the seriousness of the situation even more.

Agent Eph stood beside Plateeney on the right side and wrote notes as he started questioning this entity. It seemed to settle her thoughts a bit.

The Entity was leaning back, playing with the edges of her hair, which was long and black. As she did this, she enjoyed being interviewed as though she was egotistic, as I mentioned. The more Plateeney asked questions, the more the Entity seemed interested she was being asked.

The Entity was sexually turned on while being questioned. As the interrogation continued, the Entity moved its body from left to right in the sitting chair. It then wiggled its hips a little as though it was turned on the more it was asked.

Plateeney wondered why the Sexual Entity moved in this manner and turned briefly, giving a slightly questionable look to Agent Eph.

Plateeney wanted to see if she also noticed this.

Agent Eph just continued to look in awe. She didn't realize that Plateeney sensed this entity was manipulating the situation. The Entity continued this as much as she could.

She was trying to zone in on the interrogator's frequencies mentally. The Entity was acutely aware that she had no authority to do so.

Plateeney continued to look back at Agent Eph to ensure she was OK. He did not know what this Entity could do, so he continued asking questions.

Plateeney changed pace and asked questions to see the entities' reactions. Plateeney smiled and slowly asked, "Whenever you decide to hunt as an entity, how can you put yourself inside a human body?" "How can you manipulate a person's body (vessel)?" He sat slowly back in his chair with confidence.

The Entity smiled at Plateeney and said, "It's not hard. I sit where I choose and find whatever human female I can. I am not picky." She continued, "I don't attach myself to males much. Whenever I am forced to attach to a male, it's much harder for a man to persuade a female, which is why I dislike it."

Plateeney and Agent Eph glanced at each other. While looking back at her, the two realized this was a sexual entity that enjoyed hunting.

The Sexual Entity continued, "As women, it's easier to see because men are easier to manipulate. I can move my body while emitting a silent frequency as the victim of choice looks around. I hope to attract my victim."

As this conversation continues, The Sexual Entity explains that she will sit at the bar waiting if she is in a bar. If the Entity realizes the attraction is not taking place in the host's body that she is in, she will try to be excused to the bathroom.

The Sexual Entity manipulates them through the eyes. It is there that she will regroup her thoughts to see why. This will help them discover how to open up to those who may look at them. She also can feel the frequency of what her victim is feeling.

The Sexual Entity explained many things.

If a person is drinking alcohol, it is much easier to manipulate. The Sexual Entity, by choice, enjoys doing work solely by herself. She can communicate with other Alcohol Entities, whatever the alcohol is in. Actually, they can combine their efforts to feed off of the host.

This Entity does not prefer to be with over one host, but they will if they have to do so. The Sexual Entity added that this can escalate, especially if there is no one in the establishment of choice for her to feed on that night.

The Sexual Entity states that the easiest way to manipulate a human is by attaching to a female prostitute. This sexual practice is the vice that human stays attracted to. This Entity explains, "It's the easiest, most fun, and we make money on top of it for our host."

Suppose the female host gets arrested and gets into trouble. In that case, The Sexual Entity can transfer itself from the human host. It will usually wait for another host to attach when it shows itself.

The Sexual Entity does not mind creating danger for the host they take on. She explains that whenever the entities' actions go forward successfully, the Entity can sit back into a host, waiting for another day of the total completion. This completion is the chosen period for transfer. It could be another host showing itself.

It is all about the survival of The Sexual Entity. When in control, this entity has no mercy for the host and will not have an issue sacrificing the host to survive.

The Sexual Entity is now enjoying her words to Plateeney and Agent Eph. She sits back in the orange chair and speaks openly.

"When a male inserts his penis into a woman's vagina, it opens the crown of the top of the man's head. When this happens, the host opens all of his secret inhibitions."

She continued, "Random thoughts with his children, family, and other situations are easily readable, like frequencies as the thoughts pour as memories."

This makes it easy for The Sexual Entity to manipulate a host again if she sees him in the future or at another current time. This is excellent information for discussion.

*The Sexual Entity does not believe in the same destiny that a human does. Still, as this entity leaves the host, the action is part of the subconscious. This delivers the host the energy of negativity into the psyche. This can allow The Sexual Entity to be attached to her victim's subconscious without the victim's consent for a later date.

*This power over the host will eventually be challenged and dealt with the more contact they have. The only way an entity will not manipulate a host is simply by not being recognized. This is unlikely, but The Sexual Entity will find a new host if possible. If the host does not drink alcohol, they may be harder to manipulate. A host not joining in for attachment to this entity is not likely. This is a higher possibility if they are usually in the environment. It makes survival for the Entity very probable and much more possible. The Sexual Entity will not give up without a fight. The energy is indeed programmed to win at all costs.

The Sexual Entity explained the process and challenged the point that she could manipulate Plateeney, possibly as a personal challenge.

When Plateeney realized what this entity was trying to do, he looked back at Agent Eph as she took notes. He noticed Agent Eph wrote personal info the whole time and had glasses on her face.

Plateeney knew she could not see the Entity moving much. He figured Agent Eph did not think she could manipulate us during interrogation.

As Plateeney understood the Entity's intentions in front of them, he worried. He thought about their safety in the small, confined area.

This Entity's mission is to neurologically take advantage of the neural pathways of the host's brain. This Sexual Entity can create a Frequency through her eyes and mouth whenever she speaks. This Entity can also change its smell if needed. This is part of the feeding process, and The Sexual Entity will not stop until it finds an area to attach to a host.

Drugs make it easier for The Sexual Entity to make an advancement. If a host does the drug "crystal meth," this Entity can control their eyes and the way the eyes focus on things. This is especially true when mixing medicines with alcoholic substances.

Communication with the brain is its favorite thing to do. This Entity can create your worst fears right before you while you are on the drug. You may never have a clue if it's real or not accurate. They create an altered state of reality and wait for you to be in a neurologically changed form. When the mindset is changed, they can feed off of the manipulation.

When you fear things, they work with the other Entity. This is part of the frequencies within the drug meth.' It is no different than a hookworm or a parasite. These entities are programmed for this environment, and they enjoy their jobs. They combine their efforts to feed the host equally to push your obsessive addiction.

This is because many parasites lay their eggs during & before the entire moon cycle. During complete moon phases, you will see them a lot more. It would probably be a good idea not to drink whenever this occurs. You don't want to relapse or think you are in control if you are in rehab.

This will be a massive mistake, especially if you drink alcohol or other foreign substances. It is usually best to follow this practice at least four days after a full moon because they are always out looking for the host. But they are usually looking at all times.

{Back to The Sexual Entity trying to manipulate Plateeney}

Somehow, while in this room, Plateeney activated a green sphere. This area surrounded Plateeney and Agent Eph in time. A white field covered the green one and could wrap around Agent Eph and Plateeney.

This Entity was unsuccessful in trying to get inside Plateeney's brain.

The fascinating thing is that she tried. This happened even though this Entity was in protective custody and not allowed to do so; she did it anyway.

The Sexual Entity proves that this Entity will not show mercy when feeding. It also shows that this Entity will probably attach herself to a person with a massive ego. I observed this from her testimony as targeting individuals who enjoy drinking more. Drinking alcohol usually releases more confidence in a person's drinks. In some, the higher confidence level can also be observed as a top form of egotism.

This is a good observation because of the extreme obsession with this Entity. Here, The Sexual Entity shows the personality of an obsessed hunter who enjoys its sport.

But you must remember her sport is also a part of survival.

Entity 2

THE ALCOHOL ENTITY

As Plateeney & Agent Eph walk through the next room, they encounter a very nervous and shaky guy who does not know precisely what is happening. He is quiet while standing in a corner, unsure what to say.

The Alcohol Entity visually is a skinny male. Still, another aspect of its personality is also a larger guy, actively twitching and spastic. It's like energy flowing 100 mph but very twitchy.

This Entity is not comical, though, similar to a neighbor down the hall with a lot of nervous energy. —just a critical interpretation of a man with an undetermined possibility for much power.

One way to describe him is to explain being under the influence of alcohol. Some may say that time is the only thing that eliminates alcoholism. It's like he is coming & going like a blur of energy. It's like a wave that comes and goes in a sequence.

This Entity is there one second, and he's gone the next. The shaky process is like a short fissure between a frequency. It's like a holographic frequency there one second and gone the next. This can be similarly visualized as receiving static in a television program and losing the signal.

The Alcohol Entity is basically just inconsistent, shaken, and utterly nervous. He stares into the air briefly, then walks a bit closer from the corner wall he is standing on.

He tries to relax and have a seat, but he is just sitting at a desk, waiting for us to speak to him. He is clearly confused. The Alcohol Entity does not know what to say and remains quiet. He is radically shaken, soulless, and lost.

He is very unsure of himself and has nervous energy. His thoughts are scattered when he is spoken to. He looks around nervously, giving you the vision of a man who does not know what is happening around him.

Imagine a man sitting at a desk, confused and not knowing where he is going. He is just there existing. Every three to five minutes, his arm just twitches or creates a spasm.

A tremendous amount of nervous energy surrounds the Alcohol Entity. His physical appearance is a mixed reality or personality. You never really know what he will do or how he will react.

Plateeney and Agent Eph realize they can sit down and have a direct conversation with this being in a chair because he will not run away.

Plateeney immediately senses that this Entity is scared and will not run away. He can feel that he will not run away because of fear. The Entity will not try to be manipulative. The alcohol entity is directly connected to his host but, in time, lingers because his existence (signal) comes and goes after a time. This will be explained more.

Plateeney asks The Alcohol Entity how he can manipulate a human subject.

The Alcohol Entity is nervous and starts sweating.

He apparently does not want to share this information. The alcohol entity has a very cowardly persona about himself. He starts looking at Plateeney and then starts looking around the room. He is very insecure and dislikes being in a room with other entities.

He is very anxious about himself and tries to ensure he answers a question no one hears. He is pretty nervous about speaking.

{Brief explanation: Every Entity is on its own, but imagine you have an alcohol entity that happens to be manipulated by sex or a sexual entity. Mixing the two, you will have a person who regrets having sex because this is precisely what the alcohol entity does the next day. The sex leaves the regret, and the two will be mixed.}

Example: Say you get an STD because you were drunk, not thinking clearly, and the Alcohol and Sexual Entities were working together against you simultaneously. The next day, you will feel regret and pain that will not leave you for quite a while unless you receive trauma treatment or counseling. So basically, when working together, the two will always know they impress an endless combination of feelings that have left their 'mark' on you.

Agent Eph states: "The Alcohol Entity and the Sexual Entity should be pretty close when working together?"

Plateeney states: "Well, they are close, but they would much rather work alone. When they have to share, they are not getting a full meal. It's the way that they look at it."

Here is another example: The alcohol entity, after their briefing, starts to calm down a bit but slowly starts to look more at Agent Eph. He shows a gesture like he wants to speak to Agent Eph. After being asked three times, he seemed ready to answer questions if prepared to proceed.

Plateeney senses Agent Eph is less intimidating to him to start the process. The alcohol entity can sense that Agent Eph possibly had the taste of a drink the night before, which he is very intrigued about. So he waits for his first words as this coward sits at the edge of his chair.

The alcohol entity started to stare at Agent Eph blankly. This Entity is hoping she will be his friend. He began to feel like maybe she would be more compassionate about who he was because the taste of alcohol was within 18 hours in her bloodstream.

Plateeney spoke directly to him: "Look, talk to us both simultaneously." He explained: "This is not a situation to try and control. It's one where you are here to listen and then give us the correct information.

Plateeney reminds the Entity that he signed up for this interrogation.

Agent Eph started to look at Plateeney, slightly wondering what was going on. This was the first time we encountered such a frequency, so we were also cautious.

At this time, he turned his head, and slowly, his body followed in our direction. He started looking at the two of us once and began to open his mouth nervously.

The Alcohol Entity expressed, "Depending on what alcohol is produced or where it is also produced. When the actual alcohol is created and put into its processing, it starts to intoxicate your body. Every process is different. OK, that's why if you were bottled in, say, Mexico, you don't get the same drunk feeling...not everybody feels the same on the same alcohol. This is done on purpose."

The reason is that they would not be allowed to create what is done to them if it were the same.

Because you have tried new drinks and sampled new alcohol, you know it's different. It's not boring; it's like trying six mixed drinks in an hour.

Imagine sampling a buffet of different foods, just a different process. It's liquid, and you know it will make you feel a certain way faster or slower. If you do a quick shot, it's much more alcohol at once. It may or may not be, but it's slowly affecting your body. The faster you drink, the quicker you disconnect from your soul. The slower you drink, the more gradually you disconnect from your soul. But no matter how it happens, matter how slow or fast you do it, you still can create trauma. If you blackout, that is a trauma; we know that as entities.

When you have a trauma and your body gets sick, a slow injury in your brain occurs. What happens is like a scanning process of your body trying to leave imprints.

The imprints of the alcohol, etc., if they leave too many marks, you will be turned off and won't want another of that kind. But it's done for another reason.

For example, Plateeney thought about people taking shots or doing too many of one kind and saying I'm never doing that shot again, but I'll do this one.

The imprints are still there from wanting alcohol. The impulses and cell memory are just being changed, but it's slightly manipulated to want something else.

The more you crave, you may do it again with another kind of alcohol, and they may still do it, but the craving never repulses you.

Most may want another type of alcohol or try a new drink. But as you do this, it's a more gradual disconnect from the soul, the vulnerable state where the Entity wants to get your body. Because the more you have these cell memories and the more processes cross meridians through the body, it becomes known as a liquefied frequency. The same way your blood is. As the alcohol continues to travel through your bloodstream, it also tells your bloodstream what to do. So, it's a potent entity because it will make you think you are perfectly normal.

Then, it will show you that your body may shut down. You could have gone to sleep while you were driving. Perhaps you hit someone while you were moving, thinking you had control to drive? No matter what, you don't reflect on your life, which is why the disconnect from your soul was there because you could not allow yourself to do that.

Agent Eph states that it makes sense because when you drink the looser, you get it's like a slow trap. Plateeney says when you think that you are "not shy" because you have had two drinks, that is probably the point where you should stop.

When the alcohol entity knows that it has another 30 minutes. If you take another drink before, it tries to disconnect you from your soul at that moment.

Agent Eph states yes, just about when you jump on the Karaoke stage. Plateeney states, But the serotonin level... when it goes up, and you feel confident, it starts disconnecting at this moment, but YOU feel good.

You react in the sense that "I feel awesome. How could it not be me," yet you start singing karaoke and feel like you are the best singer in the world. The next day, you realize that was not the case. Slowly, you start to replay many questions: Did I dance? And the next day, you see yourself dancing on a video and ask yourself, why did I do that?

You don't look like the only fool. But it's OK because you are in a group, and everyone else is doing it too. But slowly but surely, this is how they can follow through with their mission.

Basically, if you have a group of people that disconnect from the soul, the more and more you continue to do this. They will stay with your cell memory... It's not going away. If you drink alcohol daily and connect your soul for 21 days... it will be a habit.

They are the most lingering entities. It can stay with you for three years with the lingering process.

Agent Eph asks the Entity a question about people who occasionally drink "occasionally," not daily but once a month. Is it just as harmful if a person gets a "buzz"?

The Entity states that it can be with an example of why you receive a breathalyzer test, and it's still at a low state of alcohol consumption. The reason is that even in that small state, it can make your body do things it's unaware of.

The alcohol entity also gave her another example. How much morphine does it take to numb you in the hospital? And how long does it take to get you there?

Think about the doses. A minimal amount and not very long at all is the answer. Another thing to consider is if you take a small pain pill (low gram amounts), like 3 grams or 5 grams or minor gram amounts, and look at what they can do to your entire body. If you were to receive an injection of alcohol, it would do a lot of harm to you, and that's why it's a frequency that comes and goes, and you are dehydrated, and then your body is drained.

If the alcohol could not do anything to you, you would never get dehydrated. As it flows through the bloodstream, it weakens the positive things in your body. This allows your immune system to heal...basically, it takes all of that away, and you get dehydrated. There is no reason why you would get dehydrated if it were positive. And that starts shutting your organs down.

Agent Eph mentions to Plateeney and the Entity that it makes sense. There could be a massive manipulation with world advertising from images on TV and the Internet that portray alcohol, painting a picture of a social drinker.

Many introverts may be shy, saying, "Have a beer look; you can loosen up and calm down and be a part of the group and get the edge off, and it's OK because you are stressed."

Plateeney states that getting a massage would be better; it releases negativity in your body. You will remove the negativity just from that.

Agent Eph states, But what about the situation after everyone forms? What are we going to do? Let's go get a drink after work on Friday.

Plateeney states, but here is the thing. If you go after hearing this information, you will not get as drunk as you used to because your brain has awareness it didn't have before.

Your soul is learning information. Suppose you allow yourself to be taken over after hearing this information. In that case, you are allowing yourself to possibly hurt yourself. It's your free will to decide after it learns and processes.

The alcohol entity states... At that point, you probably have more issues you didn't know you had, and you may be someone with a lot more aggression than you have been trying to suppress before or during childhood. These are things that you may not be aware of. These problems are things you may not have wanted to deal with.

As Entities, we receive programming to know that these things may be there, and that is where we are supposed to travel or "attach to" because that is our programmed "job."

We need to survive the most or feed directly the most. So, if we know you have a direct mechanism against us. We cannot do much because we won't allow ourselves to get to where our soul is not controlled. So you may stop yourself where you know that you need to stop. It's like you are your own guide.

Agent Eph states she has a younger acquaintance, around 21 years of age, and she has never consumed alcohol. She asks if there are tricks the Entity will do to get someone innocent who has never had a drink of alcohol to try to start. Or do they try to move away from those and go more to the weak ones?

The Entity states that if there is a group of people and your friend is next to you not drinking, we will try to dig in to get that other person involved in the fun. Suppose we have a group of individuals under the influence disconnected from their souls. You can manifest things in the same way. In that case, we can manifest the same style and feed negatively through you.

Suppose we have seven entities working through seven other individuals in a group. In that case, we can create more energy between us, which is a euphoric effect.

Agent Eph says that's why someone can get sloppy drunk, and after five beers, they are still doing shots.

The Entity states. Yes, it's more euphoric for us. It will make us feel quite well because we know you will jump and return if you get killed or hurt someone else. We can still be there.

Agent Eph says, do you stick with the same human body? Or do you float around?

The Entity states that there is an entity in every bottle of alcohol. So, if a container exists, we are there at any time. We can't transfer ourselves from one person to the next; the person has to take us in.

Agent Eph: How does an alcohol entity get inside the human body?

Is it through the actual alcoholic drink? Or do you get to the human body and convince them to get the alcohol?

Alcohol Entity: Once we are there, we are dormant for three years; we are the one that is probably in your system for the longest time. It's not a big one to share, so we don't mind sharing that space. But as you know, when you drink or want a cigarette, we both go to the place of the brain that immediately turns your "want" on.

We go to the fastest part of the soul, disconnecting the brain to directly communicate where the mind is. We can trigger that because of the cigarette's triggering cravings. We know because of the cigarette...., it will make you drink even more.

Agent Eph: What do you suppose makes the difference between someone who becomes a full-blown alcoholic and a social drinker? Alcohol Entity: See, we don't think about the term alcoholic. It's not essential.

Agent Eph says, well, someone that drinks a lot.

Alcohol Entity: It's not a problem. Some people drink every day, and they may not be an alcoholic.

Agent Eph: Well, if they are drinking alcohol, functioning fine, and are drinking alcohol every day without a personality shift. I know people like this, and I wonder what you can tell me about this situation.

Alcohol Entity: They think it's completely normal...They can believe it's OK, but your tolerance will eventually catch up with your organs. Because you are so accustomed to being that person that when you have to have a liver transplant when your organs start shutting down, you can't drink, which will piss you off. It will eventually happen and hurt you even more when it happens. This will bring on anger. It will allow other entities to come in and feed; that is how you will see others show up in time.

The best thing to do if you are going to drink is just to drink one glass. Only drink up to two drinks. If you can... drink one drink, and you drink once a year, then that's it.

Because if you drink wine every single night...Wine is one of those situations where you know it has alcohol in it....you have to drink a good bit of it to believe that you won't be disconnected, but when it makes you go to sleep.

You can't enter dream states that you can when you are sober. So it puts you in a pattern of always thinking that it's "OK," but it will affect the parts of the brain that deal with anger. So you may get pissed off at something a lot faster.

You can't get to those states of sleep healing those parts of your brain.

Agent Eph: It also makes someone more emotional.

Alcohol Entity: Yeah, another thing that happens... one of the reasons... I want to clarify the term spirits outside of a liquor store.

It's one of those things where you know that the obsession entity may be lurking... It's posted if you have a gambling problem; call this number.

We always post that there could be an effect on us.

Walking into a liquor store, you see the term "spirits." That's why we post that we are the Entity. What is a spirit? Is it an Entity?

It's no different than anything else you know in life. It is in plain sight outside the liquor store...you see it.

You really just don't think about it.

Agent Eph says, "Wow, I guess it makes sense. I had a question, but I just lost it."

Alcohol Entity mutters, "Haha, you are tired."

Agent Eph says, "Yes, it may come back to me. I am not sure if you can share this. I guess it would be kind of a remedy. But say if a full-blown alcoholic has issues and is having a hard time because it's been programmed in their mind for years versus someone who can just go out and have a casual drink and be fine."

"What's the remedy to help those people with a deep alcohol problem?"

Alcohol Entity says, "The only thing that I know that will affect a person is to make them not want the Entity or the drink. I call it the Entity because that's really what you are doing. You really are craving the alcohol entity in this state. There are three states. There's one, and it's hypnosis. The second is light acupressure daily, and the third is not drinking."

What you need to do is remember the first time you ever drank. When you remember the first time you ever drank, you look at the meridians of where those cell memories in your body are implanted that the alcohol may have touched. That makes you remember that you want it.

As you do this, you have to find them all, and when you see them all, you can basically use acupressure to find the troubled meridians in the body.

You have to pinpoint the memories and all the triggers that have made you want alcohol from the beginning, too.

When you release these memories, you can start to heal. If you use hypnosis, you will go back in your mind to remember the first time you drank.

Remember everything about how it made you feel...and everything about memories of the way and excitement of you getting there. And that's one of the significant issues when you are 21; you are excited to get that drink.

You take a memory with you, so you have to release those memories to get rid of this. It's the only way it's going to work. But you don't want to remove those memories internally. So that is why you keep wanting these cravings.

Agent Eph asks, "What if you kind of trick the brain into saying this alcohol tastes so good, but I am going to replace it with the flavor of this hot sauce? You know, trick the brain?"

Plateeney says, "Well, you know hot sauce does not have an Entity, but why would you want to burn yourself in the mouth by drinking it? You know the best method is to stop."

Agent Eph asks, "Are you saying that it's not a good thing, and it doesn't taste right, so Ughh, it's hot sauce now. It's not this tasty alcoholic beverage?"

Alcohol Entity mutters, "You can't trick your brain into believing hot sauce is alcohol. There is no Entity in hot sauce...there is no manipulation method. That's why it's powerful. Another Entity is the only thing that can mess with you and make you do something different. If there is no Entity present, you will still want it.

Here is an example: You know sugar may work because sugar is closely related to an Obsession Entity.

Agent Eph looks at Plateeney and the alcohol Entity and says it isn't that sugar is an Entity.

Alcohol Entity shrugs and says, "It's not that sugar is bad; it's probably the weakest Obsession Entity out there. We see it as the Entity stepchild, but if you are unhappy, you create sickness and sugar feeds disease, making you want us more. You drink, do drugs, or maybe more, and bring on more Entities. This allows us to feed on you the more you enter these environments. We actually want you in these environments. So, how do you deal with the bad news if you are unsatisfied? It's what it's all about."

Agent Eph says, "I'm sure they hang out at bars."

Alcohol Entity says, "Well, I would say "seedy" bars by definition. If you have a bar, that is... well, we are in every bar, but if you have alcohol or liquor, we are in it."

Agent Eph says, "OK, where are famous places we may not know you are located?"

Alcohol Entity slowly states, "Weddings... that's the best....half the time, that's the best time or place you just gave your 7-year-old kid or dog a beer for the first time. Champagne...Champagne toast that's number one. There's nothing better....everybody laughs and giggles about how awesome it is. Still, you can't really have a wedding without alcohol. And if you do, it's grape juice, and who wants that? The obsessive sugar entity is in that, by the way. So half the time, you might as well just drink water."

Agent Eph asks, "So... weddings... any place else? Favorite Countries or states?

Alcohol Entity thinks and says, "Umm, Weddings are number one. Fairs, Company Gatherings, and Public Gatherings: We greatly enjoy the Southern U.S. and Foreign Countries. You can only find a place with alcohol there. We are also the most critical economic stabilizer in parts of the world.

It's not a coincidence that you have a dry county. Because when communities start seeing the numbers of us grow, they try to start creating laws to govern those systems.

What's really amazing is how powerful the Alcohol Entity can be. It makes alcohol sales increase in those areas because they are programmed. Now, if they want it bad, they must buy it as a part of their routine at the grocery store locally.

It helped the liquor sales in those areas because you must get it at a specific time. If you can't, you will pay more for us and have already started drinking. You will get us somehow. You will figure out a way."

Agent Eph says, "But they have fun at sporting events, tailgating, prom, and football games."

Alcohol Entity says, "We are at everything, just about any event you can imagine, and it will continue. Everybody wants to cut loose with the Alcohol Entity until they realize it is ugly."

Agent Eph looks and states, "It seems so innocent because so many people frown upon a lot of other substances like marijuana or sexual or drug-related activities. It's not like Meth or other things; it's just alcohol; you think it's a problem. You don't really feel any guilt until seven more drinks later."

Alcohol Entity looks down and says, "That's what we want you to feel, and that's why we are perfectly legal. Because when you smoke, you want us. When you do drugs, you want us. Usually, we are the first ones to start it all. We are the one that dies quicker when you finish us. We are inside, but we do fade away. Our imprint is still there. And then when you drink a different one, we have a new mark, so it's interesting to stick to one drink. It's easier to get rid of that system. It's a lot harder to get rid of us when you drink a lot of different beverages. Because that different imprint is there for every drink that you sample."

Agent EPH says, "So it's more comfortable with just one?"

Alcohol Entity states, "Yeah, but It's still not easier for some people. But it's still pretty hard. (Pauses) And asks Agent Eph, how do you feel?

Agent Eph asks, "About what?"

The alcohol Entity asks, "About me?"

Agent Eph shockingly says, "About you as the Entity? Um, I have never had an issue with alcohol except for social parties or drinking at home, not so much. Still, the one thing I know is it affects me emotionally. I get hypersensitive."

Alcohol Entity says, "We help you remember."

Agent Eph says, "Yes."

Alcohol Entity asks, "Do you know why? Because we want you to do something different. It's difficult for us because we have been there for so long. But if you drink one drink, I'm there briefly and can't control anything."

Agent Eph asks, "Do you go through other people? Do you kind of whisper to the friend nearby or something?"

Alcohol Entity says, "No, but once you get a little drunker, I try to whisper to you or get you to communicate with them."

Agent Eph states, "Because I never think of having a glass of wine until someone says Would you like to have a drink?"

Alcohol Entity says, "Like I said, we last longer and are much stronger when more people are around. When everyone is at the same level, it elevates what we do, but at the same time, we want you to get more imprints in your body. And we don't last long. Because we are here, we sit on the shelf and will disappear by the night's end. It is like this example. I have a family of brothers sitting on the shelf, and I want them all to get a new life."

Agent Eph says, "Any other manipulations we are not aware of? Any tricks you pull off that we need to be mindful of if we want to stay away from you?"

Alcohol Entity says, "Ummm...We know that the person we are in will outlive us because we are there one night. So, if you had to live one night, what would you experience? That sort of question you have to ask yourself. You know...Do I wanna steal a cop car? Do I wanna do this? Do I wanna rob this? All these questions go through our head when we are in yours...and when we disconnect you from your soul...we are your soul... so it's like we have free reign. It's kind of like we just broke into the theme park. Which side do we want to ride first?"

Agent Eph says, "Interesting... It's like all fear goes away... your moral compass is entirely different, yes?"

Alcohol Entity says, "Yes, but it's like breaking into the theme park and having free reign to do anything. But you still have to understand that the host (humanity) has to know how to work machinery. You can't just magically make things work....so do you know? This is why you hear information about identifying a police officer who pulled you over, and you just so happen to goof around and grab his gun...we know we are here one night... You not...we are not exactly worried about the fact that you are going to be here tomorrow. (pauses)

We just made a party for ourselves. I'm one Entity and one beer; I have two Entities. We are not exactly happy that it's our only night to be here. So we are going to drain you. We will do everything as much as possible because, once again, it is our night to live. Think of it like this...

Now we are just hanging out with somebody. I have three people who just joined the party. I got three. The bigger the party arrives, you just so happen to throw a tequila shot of whatever into the program. It's just like you invited a Spanish female to the party.

It's the same thing... when you think about it like that."

Agent Eph shrugs and says, "I see. I had a question earlier; you were nervous and shaky. What makes you nervous?"

Alcohol Entity, now quiet (breath is heavy), says, "We don't like giving out our secrets. We are being forced to. We don't like that. We also know there are other Entities present."

Agent Eph asks, "Why were you shaking so much?"

The Alcohol Entity says slowly, "I'm not exactly in use. I'm just here. You didn't drink me. I was forced to be here, compelled to live, and I'm just deleted after this. Not even a last party for the night. I'm just here against my will."

Agent Eph asks, "Is there anything else we need to know?"

Alcohol Entity looks with a half-smile and says, "Are you sure you don't want to drink me?"

Agent Eph says, "I'm sure."

Alcohol Entity says, "OK, That's it...I mean, that's enough. You got everything out of me you wanted."

Agent Eph says, "Can there be more than one Alcohol Entity simultaneously?"

Alcohol Entity states, "Yes, we encourage it."

Agent Eph asks, "So y'all are OK with sharing? Can there be 5 different alcohol entities or more simultaneously?"

Alcohol Entity says, 'Yes, it's like I said... It's like my family of brothers just showed up at the party. As many here, the better.

Think of it like this. One person is blocking a window, and a little sun comes in. As you drink... another person stands before the window and blocks more of the sun.

Imagine your soul as the sun. The more you drink, the more the sun from entering the window as people come in decreases. Once the window is closed from the light, your soul is also blocked... basically, it's the Entity's party at that point."

"It's probably the best description I can give. And what's even better is you ultimately allowed it."

Agent Eph says slowly... "Typically, is it just one or more than one?

Alcohol Entity says, "It's usually more than one unless you are 16 and weigh 80 pounds."

Agent Eph thinks and says, "Well, that is all that is coming to me at this time."

Alcohol Entity asks, "Can I go Now? (like a child)

Plateeney states, "You are free to go."

Entity 3

THE ENERGY VAMPIRE ENTITY

The Energy Vampire Entity is one Entity that can change its form (shape-shift). This Entity approaches its interrogation position as a puff of black smoke. The dark cloud moves slightly because it does not want to take on a form to reveal its identity. As it approaches the seating area, eight large blue light beams are visible to contain the Entity in its surroundings.

At this moment, the ceiling opens up, and then a light flashes brightly. This apparently sends a frequency showing the Entity that it must cooperate with the training procedure. You can see the black smoke start to move in a circular tornado pattern. The agency standards do not want this Entity to have the ability to create channeled conversations with the interrogators. A field of magnetic frequency is placed in front of Plateeney and Agent Eph before interaction.

This Entity is challenging to be around. Agent Eph is stable and ready for a possible attack from the Entity. She realizes this moment is unlike the previous two and must be prepared for sudden problematic movements.

Plateeney is observing the situation and clearly can sense the possible danger in the case. He realizes firmly that this very driven Entity does not want to cooperate. He takes a step back when he views the Entity taking on a humanoid form. At this time, Plateeney and Agent Eph see that the beams of blue light can communicate telepathically with the Entity surrounding them.

As they start to flash, Plateeney realizes that the beams are sending a message to the Entity that it has one more attempt to comply or will be terminated. The beams remind the Entity that it signed up for this occurrence. It will take matters more directly if compliance takes place after some time.

Agent Eph asks: What is your main reason for functioning?

Plateeney holds his hand and addresses Agent Eph to wait for a second. A dark cloud of smoke starts to turn green in color and then moves into the shape of what looks like a man very slowly. As the cloud grows more substantial, the visible cloud morphs into about a 45-year-old man dressed with small wire-framed glasses shaped in small circles.

This Entity looks from left to right with strangely darker squinting eyes. The Entity's eyes are tiny and sunken into the eye sockets. He takes complete form and gives off a strange pedophilia presence. His mannerism is very childlike. Plateeney can sense this is one of the secrets of this Entity that it does not want to reveal. He is not happy to have had to show his pure form.

The Entity wants us to believe he is another entity because he was forced to show himself. His hands are both on his lap. He has some weird eye twitching. There is scattered hair with a brown patch in the front, but mainly distributed on the top of the head. It's a balding look, but we know this particular Entity can and probably will morph its form as it starts answering questions. At this time, the Entity looks like a human. Plateeney is sensing that this Entity does not have an actual proper form. But he knows it's time to begin with caution.

Plateeney starts explaining briefly to Agent Eph what this Entity resembles. Just before they are about to start questioning. He asks her to imagine a guy walking around a city park at night. If you are near and see him, you immediately know something weird or strange about his presence. Still, if you ask or speak out, you may have a confrontation that may seem like the "victim" or may try to threaten you with a lawsuit. But their eyes are piercing you with various thoughts.

Another example is to be in a sales position, and you may have had a bad week. Imagine another salesperson you may work with who may approach you by asking questions like "How is your week?" "How are you feeling?" The feeling makes you feel drained, and you can barely answer the question. The strangeness of the questions makes your mind scattered, which is an excellent indication that there is a strange transfer of energy.

It starts off very confusing. Before problems start, this co-worker knows you are having a bad day and continues challenging you to ensure you have the repetitious thought of negativity. This is the vibe and sense that Plateeney was trying to describe what he felt in the Energy Vampire entity. As they started asking questions, Agent, Eph, and Plateeney knew to be on guard because they knew the Entity could quickly change shape.

The Vampirish Entity is not happy to be in the energy field he is sitting in. You can tell because an auric lot of this body has a slight shimmy whenever it thinks of negativity. There is a dark area around the field, also. This area can be controlled, and it gains its own energy. Imagine a jellyfish of smoke and a puff of smoke moving. Smoke surrounds it, moves again, and the field still encompasses it.

The Entity reads our energy fields and knows we are revealing its secrets. Because it slightly squeezes his knees every time we speak about him.

Agent Eph asks the Entity if he has tendencies and thoughts to hurt children. The Entity slowly leans forward with his hands on his knees and speaks in a cowardly soft voice the word "yes." He lets off a vibe like he is the victim you should feel sorry for. She asks: "What is your objective as the Entity you are currently? He looks at Plateeney and Agent Eph and says slowly, "Do I have to answer?"

The two interrogators look at each other and say yes simultaneously. Agent Eph rolls her eyes and moves her chair as Plateeney explains It's time for you to start talking Motherfucker. We don't have all day. The Entity looks at Plateeney with both eyes, making a "mean" face. Plateeney says Now we are getting somewhere. Both eyes squint at Plateeney's neck, sending a vibe that it wants to argue. But it knows it's vulnerable, so it's trying to relax.

The Entity knows it will probably not be able to survive this interrogation. One reason is that it withdraws a lot of energy just to speak out loud without a host or human vessel. It has to be recharged by its external auric field to show anger regularly, and when it emits too much, it starts to shake briefly. The Entity regains composure and begins to regain its strength. The Entity is quite shy; speaking takes a lot of energy. The Entity is aware it may not survive different formations. So, it would have to start talking to return to its smoked appearance. Which is the form it likes to be in to create the most energy for itself.

Agent Eph wonders if the Entity could try to take their energy, and Plateeney shares with her that he could, but the field will not allow it at this time. Agent Eph asks again. What is your primary purpose for this Energy Vampire Entity? What kind of destruction are you trying to cause when you enter a human host? The Entity speaks and says, "We were created." Eph says and... The Entity states again: "We were created.....to feed energy to send a signal back to the species that created us." Agent Eph is perplexed. She asks, "What is that species?

The Entity states that it is a draconian figure, and it has a similarity to a reptile. She then asks what the origin is. What planet? The Entity says he does not know. EPH asks why they need this energy. The Entity states, "to survive." Agent EPH asks, How do you enter the host? What kind of manipulation is done? Is it easy or difficult?

The Entity states that there is no manipulation at all. Humans are the simplest parasite-host to conquer. That's why this happens. We can sense what a human does not like about him or herself.

A person is so scared of their breath smelling. When we sense that we fear our breath smelling, we get excited and can't wait to be close to it because it allows us to survive around that energy for at least two days.

Plateeney asks...So what happens to a person when you get near them? The Entity states, "They deteriorate their own energy. Some get tired. It depends on the person's outcry of how much energy they emit at that particular time." Plateeney asks: Can you connect to a host to affect them emotionally? Why do you do this?

The Entity states we do not need to be the host; we can control an aspect of the host just by connecting to its auric field. We also know there may be other entities present inside the host. We don't enjoy sharing energy too much, so we always wait to see what the body reveals before exploring all aspects of possibility.

It is easier when another entity is present because the body already has an object. This is easier because we just move in where the other left off. We actually enjoy this more. Agent Eph asks, "What happens to the human personality?" The Entity states,,, Slowly but surely, some of them may start to feel that there is something wrong with them. They may feel bothered slowly or fast.

The Entity looks at Agent Eph and asks...What is depression? Agent Eph looks at Plateeney and says, well, when you feel negative thoughts. A person pretty much feels miserable. Also, you can't get out of bed, miserable, and it's tough to get out of that state of mind.

The Entity looks at Agent Eph and Plateeney and says if a person is what you say, they already have three or more entities attached. We can elevate these feelings to the maximum effort if we show up. If we turn up, then a person would have already lost their free will at that point.

They would have already allowed it to be taken or manipulated.

Plateeney asks, what is the most attractive aspect you see when you show up? The Entity states that they get tired. It says: We don't like to show up and drain a person. When we consume about 25% of the energy capacity, we may stand back after the host gets tired to ensure we don't become detected. They won't see us physically, but they may know immediately something is wrong if we react too quickly. We like to start small.

Agent Eph says she would prefer to get away from this person as quickly as she is around someone with an energy vampire entity. I can only be around them for a short time. The Entity states that when that happens, it's usually because you have an entity that knows we are doing it or (yawns slowly).

It means that if you do sense it, you will feel groggy. But mainly, people don't detect it until around a year of abuse. Here are three examples.... 1. Asking a person too many questions. And you know the answers the person does not want to answer. (pushy) (yawns again)

Imagine questions a psychiatrist would ask you to talk about your problems, and it starts to make you fatigued. Your mechanisms are not up (shields, it states). As they begin to release, then we begin to receive.

You are fully wide open. Imagine us intertwining your energy fields like a snake, and you start tired. The second you wonder if something is wrong, it's gone, and you just think you may be tired. (yawns again) The Entity says the word "imagine" with slow and slurred speech. Imagine yourself crying, and you start to feel like you are tired. We can drain your energy while you call while we enter your auric field. Plateeney asks, is it more accessible to drain a person if we are in a great mood?

The Entity states, yes, we will still try. It's a little more complicated and not as helpful because if you don't want anything to make you feel bad, you will stop the conversation and move away. Agent Eph asks, is there anything else part of the process? We make a person feel awkward, so they release emotion. She says it would be the opposite. If you make a person feel uncomfortable, why would they open up to you? The Entity states all we need is emotion. As long as you have an emotion, we can drain. Happy, sad, awkward, we can take energy after any feeling.

You see, we don't live in a host. If a person makes you feel awkward, they do not have an entity; they may be uncomfortable. So you don't know, and that's why we didn't wanna come here today.

At any time, it forces you to judge...we like judgment more than anything because it's an emotion everyone participates in. So, literally, we don't need to interweave ourselves with a judgemental person. We can just exist outside of them.

Agent Eph says OK,. Continue. OK, so you make us feel awkward, and what else? The Entity states the only emotion we don't like is sexual excitement. She says, explaining. He says temptation. We don't like that emotion. Agent Eph says, So you don't like the sexual Entity? He says if we see a sexual entity in or lurking near us, we stay away unless we are near death. We are comfortable if they are there. We don't hang out with any of them. They don't even know we are there. We are not usually detectable by many entities.

Agent Eph says: I thought you stated that you are comfortable with them and easier. Regarding the entity status, we are pleased if they are for you, but we don't mess with a human if they are out there looking for a host and see that they are just getting in there.

The reason why is because that particular Entity is learning everything about that human. It's getting to know you. So if we come around, they will know something is wrong because the energy will change. Imagine something showing up and attaching itself to your brain, and then imagine that another point comes and attaches itself to your auric field. Your auric area is like a shield, but it's energy.

Suppose you set up a mechanism that something is bothering you. It will tire us if we get into that energy or do something within it. It can make you feel drained, and then you know it's horrible for that Entity.

In that case, the Entity is unhappy because it tries to kick it out. So if it knows we are there, it proceeds to kick us out, and it's not good for us.

Plateeney asks, Is it more accessible to feed off of women or men? The Entity States Women are highly emotional; we will quickly provide a female. Men are not so sensitive...some are. The whole thing about men is that they seem able to pick up on problems faster because women are emotional quite a bit. If a woman feels something is wrong, she thinks something is wrong with her. If he thinks something is wrong, the man just goes the other way.

Agent Eph asks if it messes with the mind and tries to create the human person to build negative stories that spiral to lower the energy. The Entity states We automatically reduce your energy. But what would be the benefit of messing with the mind? Say she's horny...we don't like sexual energy, so we would immediately try to change her mind about being horny.

Agent Eph asks: Are there any other times you would try to mess with our head? We may create a problem that she needs to think about. We can break the feeling if she has a thought or an emotion. The Entity states they can break up our chakras.

Agent Eph says, explain chakras. The entity status chakras are points in the body that are quite colorful....when you have a higher vibration as a human, you will see color. Then, there will be a better alignment.

We try to knock you offline because if you get offline, you will not question how you feel so much you will just do it. You are not going to worry about a massive amount of energy. You will just react to what you are told. If we break your alignment of the chakras, your emotions will be everywhere. Which is what we like.

When you are more emotional, it is easier to pull the energy from a person.

Agent Eph states: How long does a person take to regain power? The Entity said slowly and scattered (weak). It depends on what they are around or doing. Humans are the only creatures on Earth that don't understand their energetics. Sometimes, they may never get it back. If they know what chakras are, they stay aligned. And they will keep feeding us any time one comes around. We keep feeding their energy. Because they are constantly emotional. Agent Eph asks if they have the knowledge and do the work and learn about energy vampires or something similar.?

Entity explains: We will only be around them briefly if they have a lot of expertise. Would it be possible to regain their energy so they can recharge? The Entity states Sleep is the only way you can restore. Agent Eph says: You say they may never get it back? But everybody sleeps, so would they get it back naturally?

The Entity says yes to a human. It does, yes. But if their chakras need to be aligned, they will only get it back if they understand. They would have to realign. When a person has deteriorated, the alignments are more challenging to get back. Religion in a human is very controlling.

Depending on their belief system, people are either easier to feed on or more complex to live off of. Suppose a person goes within themselves or meditates to vibrate higher frequencies inside their DNA. It's hard to feed on people like this because they close off the auric field to any external energies trying to come in.

I'm telling you that if your chakras are misaligned, you need to know what a chakra is. They stay misaligned; you may become accustomed to your chakras being misaligned and get used to that.

Agent Eph asks: So the more a person has intimate knowledge and a higher vibration with positive emotions (with understanding), do you still try? Can they affect a person's life or the loss of a job? An entity will try anything it can. It may be more challenging, but they will still try. If someone is vulnerable next to the person they are trying on, they may move away from the stronger-willed person. But it does not mean they are prejudiced against the individual; they prefer a more accessible target. (yawns twice)

Plateeney looks at EPH and states I need to inform you that the Entity is losing a lot of energy. Agent Eph says, OK. Plateeney says they don't stop feeding. They always provide, but I'm letting you know he is getting drained. The Entity is doing to himself what they do to others, and he is being forced to. It's OK if he does not morph right before you. Also, another weird thing was he almost turned into a frog, and the light beings told him no because he couldn't speak. Agent Eph says, Why a Frog? It was easier to survive because it's a more diminutive form.

Eph asks the Entity again if they can lower their vibration to bring hardships in people's lives.

The Entity states, "It's not that we cause it. We drive you to be emotional, so as we come and go, you are the one doing it. We are just stimulating it. Our primary goal is to keep you off balance. Eph angrily states: So why not allow us to regain our energy? The Entity says: We move forward because we don't attach ourselves to one person. It's to feel that energy. It's a field that exists inside the area of strength. Suppose you are high on power or vibration, walking around in love, and suddenly, you are way off track and in a car accident. In that case, you may have somehow manifested that accident. Still, realistically, it could have been the idea that two different energies were transferred. You may have revealed the accident. But not the rapid pace; you just didn't know there was more than one energy simultaneously.

Why would you care if you caused chaos in someone? We don't care. We are doing what we are programmed to do. There is no sense in being around you when you are healing because we know it is much better for us the next day. If we know that you have a natural sleeping pattern, we will show up at the same time every day to make you feel like there is something wrong with you other than us. That way, you need help figuring it out. But we can be in your office and feed off the whole office. If you have an entire room that is dramatic and bouncing off the walls with emotion, then we are probably there somehow.

Plateeney asks: What will immediately make you leave a room? The Entity states when a person feels finished and has closed off their energy. Then we are done. We may come back around here and now. But if we stay, it just makes you angrier. When you emit frenetic energy, you have an interesting thought. We can set you up for other entities if you get more upset. So when you are done with us, and we leave, we have a brother that can step right in. This is why being aware of and educated about energy is essential.

When skeptical people say terms like "that is a new age," we enjoy that because that just aggravates the person. They know they are not making it up. It's a situation where we exist. Our brother lives, and we do what we need to survive and store energy to send back to our creator. The "creators" are unhappy as I sit here because I am not returning energy. Many people think a reason for survival is going to school, working, raising kids, etc. Still, my right to survive is to send energy. It's what I'm programmed to do. It's not positive energy. I can post it somewhere when you create power and survive off of some.

Many humans think they know what this is. Many people feel they know how to get rid of the problems, but realistically, it's getting rid of my creator. That's the issue because if my owner does not exist, neither of us lives. My brother entities, but we have different objectives. I have an existence that allows me to feed off positive and adverse energy but not sexual energy. Another entity does that, and they need to work for my creator. So here's the thing. All of them create something and allow us to continue what we do. So we don't care what everyone else does. We don't care about the human, the host, or anything. We have a job, and we get it done. This is what we are programmed to do.

Agent Eph says: 'So it's like building a house. First, there is a frame, then sheetrock, etc.'

The Entity states: Yes, that is similar to what you mean, one after the next working together. We are like a surveillance camera of energy and can do this to animals. It does not matter if you have a soul or not; you just have to be living.

Agent Eph asks: What is your original form? He says a foggy gas. She then asks: Does it smell? He says no, it is primarily grayish-black in color, and you can't see it in your standard dimension.

Agent Eph asks: Why did you pick this form?

The Entity states: I didn't. My creator chose my style ultimately.

Agent Eph continues: Do you feed your creator energy?

The Entity says yes, and it goes into a harnessed energy generator.

Agent Eph: It just keeps him or them alive?

The Entity says: Yes, that's why we were programmed and created. We can't say no, or we will not move forward to our creator.

Agent Eph: You are about to die, so you can tell me everything. Have you ever not wanted to be an entity?

The Entity states: We are not programmed in that way. We do not have a soul, and neither does my creator. They don't feel happy. They are more interested in problems here and a negative state because they know it creates a survival method for us. My creator is active in your government on Earth and can be he or whatever form they feel they need to take on. Sometimes both. But we need to find out how they do this.

Agent Eph: Do you have more than one creator?

The Entity says, no, we do not.

Agent Eph: He is a significant influence in the political world on Earth and goes into a physical human form to create chaos in disguise.

The Entity shares that this can bring more negative energy to you as a person creates positive and negative energy. Your soul somehow controls the body to produce both of these energies. The power they are primarily concerned about is negative energy. When they harness my point, they only take the negative energy. I get what's left, which is the positive energy if it's there.

I must be aware of bringing positive energy also. When I am harvested by my creator, I will die if I only get negative energy, and they take it all.

I must harness some positive power to survive that process.

In the same way, you feel drained at the end of the day because you think you have worked all day or fed off of it. They do the same thing to the rest of the world because they only care about negative energy. I feed off negative emotions, but they take that from me, and I live off the other emotions. You create and live off of two energies. Both your negative and positive energies create a light source. Imagine positive energy makes light. The negative energy creates a light, too; it's just a different energy. Both of them create a light source. When you establish both of these energies, I can harness that energy. We can leverage both, but they know how to filter it as fuel. Energy is energy, but positive and negative energy are entirely different.

Agent Eph asks: Does it matter what kind of energy you get?

The Entity goes on: Like I stated, They want me to mainly get negative energy, but if I can't, they will figure out a way to get more.

Usually, if I have to stay around a particular area, I like to be around all energies. One example is if I get nothing but negative energy in a day, they choose to take it from me. I will die if they handle all the negative energy they want. I need strength to survive, and they take the negative from me, so I will die if I only get the negative energy.

Agent Eph asks: Are you deteriorating from me asking these questions?

The Entity says: I am at 25% as a source.

Agent Eph states: So I better ask everything I need; you're in the red zone. The Entity says: I don't understand.

Agent Eph: It's a joke, like a phone when it's close to a dead battery. It is an expression we say. Anything else that we need to know?

The Entity: The energy field that surrounds me so that I cannot drain your energy was created by my owner, so I don't understand how to use it.

Agent Eph: Hmm, that's interesting (pauses). Anything else? What percentage are you now? The Entity says I'm still at 25%, but I don't want to reveal anything. It's better when you ask.

Plateeney asks: The energy that surrounds you is created by your owner; what kind of energy is it exactly?

The Entity says: It's an energy that exists around the Earth. It is like a containment.

This power is slowly deteriorating because forces outside your planet are trying to stop these hidden powers from taking place. Some forces outside the globe do not precisely like my creator and do not want them to leave. To leave, they are trying to detain them; they do not wish to escape your world or start over somewhere else.

Much of the planet is surrounded by this same energy. Outside external forces don't want them in other parts of the universe. And yes, my creator has created this energy.

It has been reversed and used against them recently, which had to come from a government above the planet or one unseen on Earth.

Plateeney asks: Does music affect you?

The Entity says: Yes, any time a frequency is emitted with no emotion, like a song or a Gong, it throws us off balance. Imagine all light is energy, so the light comes in when you open the blinds. When you close the curtains, tiny traces of light come in. You can't see this with the human eye, but when you play music or play a lot of frequencies, the frequency being emitted or the vibrations on these instruments can shut down the entities for a little while.

Agent Eph asks: Is there any music that you are attracted to? The Entity immediately looks around and says that it does not attract music. If anything, music could be our enemy. Agent Eph: So it's like your garlic to a vampire?

The Entity: Yes, I think so. Sometimes, we can't run away because the frequency comes on and goes through us. Agent Eph, which is treasured information, is the most I have heard. The Entity states: It's like protection only for some entities because not all entities are affected by frequencies. Some do, and others do not affect the host's body. So, it is like a form of protection.

The entities that need a host, for example, entities, are shielded by the body they are in from being affected. A person may hear one of them not happy about a particular frequency. Still, the body is addicted to a specific frequency only.

Agent Eph asks: Is there any noise you dislike besides music? The Entity says, "Any noise we don't like, any frequency at all, any sound at all. There is nothing we like; that's why when you scream and say enough, it's a very similar frequency."

Agent Eph: So you don't like sexual energy or music? The Entity says we don't know what sexual energy is...but we also don't like the current lights around me. As well as light energy because I can't feed. It's not positive or negative; it's just light energy or something else I could provide.

Agent Eph: Anything else? The Entity looked around slowly and said: My owner or creator can sometimes make us leave a place. One example is by playing music in confinement all the time. We don't try to continually be near people who do something positive or keep positivity around. We feed off positive energy, but if we don't pick up a trace of negative energy for our creator, we don't usually keep going around there. Because ultimately, he wants negative energy. We will not regularly be around someone or an environment with a positive vibration or energy.

Here is where it gets interesting, though, because I am almost about to fade away. Not everyone will have a perfect day, so we were created to track it. And one more thing, we don't like sexual energy, but our creator loves it. The "creator" can sense somehow that we are around sexual energy. If it's problematic sexual energy, they will ask for coordinates and know our location.

They can directly affect that person the most. They feed directly off of that energy the most. They enjoy that fear energy; if it's sexual fear energy, it's like a bonus for them, especially if it's traumatic fear energy. They will almost force us to. It's like one of those situations when we don't want to be there. The creator will force us to return to the location against our will.

This is usually when you are sleeping. You will have a certain amount of time while sleeping to heal. They can access you through your dreams and create frequency sexually through our location.

This process can also very rarely delete us in the process. It depends on the use of force against us. Agent Eph says: Your boss is not an entity. You are an entity, so what would your boss be called? The Entity says He has many names, but we know it to be "Archon." Plateeney asks: What percentage are you at? And how long has this been going on? Agent Eph quickly says: It's been an hour and 15 minutes.

The Entity states slowly: I am at 10%.

Plateeney says you can last about an hour and twenty minutes without energy. That means if everyone on the planet was surrounded by a positive force field around them, you could not feed at all. If this were to happen, you would all die or vanish. If this happens, what will happen? The Entity says slowly again: We would no longer cease to exist. Plateeney says: What is this energy called that surrounds you? The Entity: I don't know. I just know it does not allow me to do anything. I can't move when I feel it.

Plateeney says: So being that your boss can feed your energy...if we rid the planet of all of your kind, would it be possible to dissolve your boss off too? The Entity says: Yes, it's possible. Plateeney asks: How long is their life span without feeding?

The Entity says: Usually twenty-four hours if every human was actively positive for 24 hours. Plateeney states: So basically, if that took place?

The Entity looks up and says slowly: You would rid my creator completely off this planet. However, there is no guarantee because you must accomplish this task to test the theory. Plateeney says: This could be highly unlikely mainly because of your media, radio, and TV programs. Agent Eph says: Well, we will dismiss this interrogation if there are no more questions.

Plateeney and Agent Eph approach the door to leave the room with the now helpless Energy Vampire entity. Before Plateeney enters the door's exit, he turns around and tells the Entity: "Have a good day." Now at 3%, the Entity starts to fade into a slight white smoke. From what we have heard, this is probably the start of the deterioration of the Energy Vampire Entity.

Entity 4

THE PSYCHIC ENTITY

Today, we are speaking about the Entity of Curiosity. The whole purpose of curiosity is psychic power. It's not stating that interest is not good. Still, when you get curious about things involved in the future, the more you want to know what will happen, you lose track of your understanding of them now. You become obsessed with the "need to know this now." You think that someone can tell you what will happen. Usually, this occurs when someone is a "card reader" or tarot reader.

Connecting with guides and other skills in altered realities or dimensions into the unknown. Knowing some things is good, especially regarding mental blocks and meridians. Still, the vast majority of people sway toward money. It always goes towards material things, and this is where it can become obsessive.

Example: If someone shares in reading that you "probably" need to play video poker this weekend, and you "win," you will continue to go to this person. Your first reaction is to ask for another appointment. This can become obsessive. It can lead to being out of control or out of the ordinary, especially if they seek a fee.

Depending on their religious beliefs, some people are very skeptical about this. Agent Eph states that she has heard before that any psychic you go to is not of God or any part of it. And The Entity spoke up and said this was not the case.

Here is an example. Whenever the situation is very involved, you go to a psychic regularly. Similar to requiring a regular massage, consider it. But you have a bunch of mental blocks, and you need help with this to move forward with your mission or purpose.

If you came to a teacher wanting to know your problems, you could work together and find out how to explain the roots and aspects of the problem. In that case, this is more OK because it's helping you clear your negative blocks of karmic energy. The whole purpose is to remove problems in your life and learn about the issues.

But if you go to a teacher and say: "Where are my problems?" Then, you can be questioned to learn. Then you can work on this. I have some problems and need to find out where those problems are. Then, relax and try to feel the energy with issues within my chakras. If you can't express yourself, you probably have problems with your throat chakra. If you feel like you cannot love, you probably simultaneously have issues with your throat and heart chakra.

This is what psychic energy is used for...to clear mental blocks or help people with clogged meridian points of the body so you can be more cleared or aligned. You may not be able to see this right away, but you must be chakra-aligned in mind, body, and soul to understand where a blockage may be. Meditate tremendously or know who you are.

Understanding who you are can help you accept yourself. What is the whole purpose of a guide? This should be the first question. And if you cannot, you can ask yourself what stops you from taking yourself? You do not need someone else to answer these questions to move forward. You can look within yourself and get these answers. Ask yourself...

People look at various things as guides. The Catholic Church's followers look at a priest as a guide. In any religion, they may watch a pastor as a guide. Whoever usually stands before them in their faith is who that person is as a guide. One example could be I need your help because they believe this person may be guided by God. It's not for any other reason, but you also have psychic teachers guided by God. So, it's not that all psychic readers and educators are cynical. The word psychic is also not harmful but has negative connotations for many. But the whole purpose is not to become addicted to knowledge.

This is where people become addicted.

An example is a person who always asks questions. Example: Is my boyfriend cheating on me? Can you tell me about the cards? This may not be accurate information. Some people can manifest an issue by thinking about these things. You can go home and create a massive fight with the individual you are with. You may not know entities working there trying to build issues in your life regarding thoughts you may not feel balanced about. Open your mind as we speak to this Entity because many things will emerge. There are many strange questions and scenarios, too. But this is a learning experience to have a better gut feeling. This situation can be very addictive.

Here is an example that it can become addictive for both people involved. If you are making money primarily 100 to 200% on being a psychic, you must create a clientele if no one knows you are psychic.

They look at it as a gift;,,, it's not a gift for the rest of the world. It's a gift because you have aligned yourself properly. It's a gift because you have worked with yourself to only get to that point in your education. A problem persists because the people who come to you may not be at that point, and you have become a Messiah to them. And you are not a Messiah.

Agent Eph states: That's right! Plateeeney says: Because the people never fix anything, they just take the guidance, and eventually, they may get stuck because they never had to learn how to expand their knowledge to move forward. It's like the man who never did his laundry in a marriage of sixty years.

Example: When a man and woman are married for 55-65 years. The lady may pass away, and this man has never done his laundry once. How is he going to survive? He will have to figure out how to survive. This is similar to when someone may go to a psychic too often. Their decisions and inner gut feelings become a hidden force that cannot be learned from.

Another example is a woman who has never worked and has been a housewife for thirty years. A husband passes away with no life insurance. The woman must make rash decisions and survive at the most challenging time. This is one of the problems with our society because we find the easy way out. The easy way out is psychic. The easy way out is always asking many questions to the one who can get the answers. The easy way out is telling me how to win the lottery. Or to be able to get to a point without working towards a goal?

This is what happens. I cannot open my third eye, but you can, so why don't you tell me how to do this. This causes issues because if you continue to take on a person's karmic energy, you can take it on yourself if you clear it without them learning the outcome. It can be entirely deceitful to both people involved, in it's completely one-sided.

This could be why EFT (Emotional Freedom Technique) and Acupuncture work so well. The individual coming for assistance chooses to be there and has to physically accept what is happening to them and become a part of the sequence. You have to do it. You must stretch yourself and learn to move forward.

An example is having multiple college degrees and never implementing a field of work. You eventually have to take yourself to school and "DO" something. It's all talk until you do or create something with the study. The same thing happens in every world: the physical world, the supernatural world, the underworld, the same thing in every society. Every dimension of life has knowledge; you must learn how to move forward when you need to pass on.

This is another experience that people are afraid of and don't understand. Many don't ask a psychic what's it like on the other side? What do I need to do on the other side? What am I going to do when I die? Example from

Agent Eph: Am I going to have money? The man of my dreams, etc.? Everyone wants to know that. But I follow astrology and understand moon phases while linking your personality to your birthday. In that case, I can pinpoint your nature entirely.

You can quickly identify people by researching and learning the character cycles.

Agent Eph states: Well, what would be my personality? She says she was born on Sept 16 and is a Virgo.

Plateeney says you question yourself quite a bit more than others.

Agent Eph makes a face and says, But how do you know that.

Plateeney says Because I understand the signs.

Agent Eph says I have never read this. I do, but I also question other people.

Plateeney says when you interview someone, you are your most significant skeptic. Then, he learns that she is on the cusp of LEO (which can be entirely deceitful if crossed), so he states that she mixes and matches with the moon phases. Every person can be learned, and it can be worked to be a good match with a person, etc. This is not a coincidence. If it's supposed to work, it's meant to work for you. When you put too much emphasis on this cycle, you continuously keep reading and believing in these cycles. You may miss out on a perfect person because you may not listen based on something you read, which may alternatively create a wall before anything gets started. This is not a coincidence, and it's a great reason you should always look within. If it's supposed to work, it's meant to work for you. If you choose to disallow it to work, you cannot put all your eggs in that basket because sometimes you have to create things to work for yourself.

Agent Eph states, going back on her questioning in this conversation. She says most of her search is because she always looks for curiosity and teachability factors. But there are some things that I feel are complete "BS." I want to be condensed. But sometimes, I just want to believe what we discuss, but there is always something new that makes me wonder. Does this make sense?

Plateeney states, But you don't need to question yourself.

Agent Eph says, but I'm not.

Plateeney says, but you are doing it right now.

Agent Eph says, "Umm."

Plateeney states you want to ensure you don't need to question yourself. You wanna make sure that you don't need to ask yourself because you just "know" who you are.

You're saying that you make sure you don't need to question yourself and don't want to ask, but you are still asking yourself.

And given that knowledge of what I just said and what you are saying, I can manipulate you.

Agent Eph: I am not that easily used.

Plateeney says I'm telling you right now. Everyone is easily manipulated. This is why you always need to go from within. When you go from within, you are not easily controlled.

You can change that setting if someone tries to tell you who you are from your personality. The mood then sets everything about it internally. Suppose you are a person who is looking for straight abundance, very similar to what a monk looks for after ten years of silence. In that case, your personality does not make sense because you are not that person. You can literally become any character if you can do that. Only a person sitting in silence can go within themselves and see who they are.

They know if they can jump over a six-foot fence, it knows that it allows them not to be manipulated. Does this make sense? Agent Eph says, of course. Plateeney continues: You can easily be manipulated when you don't "know," which many people don't. They may be cautious because they have never done a ritual that allowed them to open up and believe what is being told. When they do some sort of ritual practice of whatever is being described, they will no longer question it because they have done the work. But it has to be a part of your subconscious.

Agent Eph states Because it makes them uncomfortable. Many people question because they don't know what they are talking about. They immediately return to the same belief system their parents taught them. It could be a part of me that wants to believe is the authentic self, and the truth is that death with a voice that is going "this is true" is trying to get in, and the ego is fighting it. Plateeney says: To me and my opinion, if you allow the ego to do anything...to me, the ego is manipulation.

Agent Eph says: Right, but then the ego is also going. The ego should not be there at all. That's why you want to look within yourself to release the ego as much as possible.

What I mean is the original data we were given? Plateeney says: Here is an example. Whenever a seven-year-old walks through the mall, the parent may tell the seven-year-old, " Don't talk to strangers, don't listen to anyone except me. If you are walking in the mall and someone says, "Come see," what do you do? You are trying to believe the personal stuff because you must return to your thoughts.

Run away and find an adult and say, "I need your help?" A lot of parents have told their children that. We were a generation where our parents said this. OK, now when you think about that concept, You know if you were that child at seven and someone walked up to you and said, hey, you need to come with me. Then you knew the feeling you got when this stranger approached you at a young age, "the nervousness." This is the same feeling that you should still feel like an adult.

And that's the truth. Stop asking for advice and look within if you don't feel it. Find the information from 'you' because if you don't believe it, you have too much ego blocking your genuine nature and your soul as one.

It's no different if someone is walking down the hallway. Agent Eph looks around and mumbles: I know what you mean. Plateeney states: But you know what I'm saying, it's a gut feeling.

You just know there is a weird vibration coming from a particular person. You just feel it. Agent Eph says that's why I thought we had an ego; it's like a fight or flight thing to help us with this stuff.

Plateeney says: I believe the ego needs a better mission. We should not have any attachments to an ego whatsoever.

Agent Eph says that determining a person's danger may be something else. Not expanding because our ego is keeping us safe.

Plateeney says: To me, the ego is not keeping us safe. It may play a role in how we react. The ego makes you swing at another person; it makes you pull someone's hair, break a bottle, and do all these things you didn't have while you were a child.

Agent Eph states: It may also talk you out of a job promotion, quit your job, or take on your own business. That's what I mean by playing it safe. Here are some thoughts

Plateeney says: "The ego is the accelerant of manipulation. It's this person you have created, an imposter, the opposite in the way of you who you will become, that you must break the wall down to not see. To move forward in life the right way.

You can be competitive without an ego. You can be driven without an ego. You can do anything in life without ego. People with less ego have more companionship.

They have more spirituality and more relaxing time with themselves. They don't care whether you go to a man's or a woman's night out... they can trust. They drop all of those negative emotions that create controversy.

They know if something happens, there is a logical explanation of why, or they just don't need to be in this situation anymore. When you release the ego, that is it.

I have had many people ask or discuss me as an example: What would you do if you walked into your wife having sex with another person? What would you do? I would probably say after taking a picture, OK, have a good day. Tomorrow, we can discuss how to move forward. Many people say I don't know if I could react like that. To do nothing seems crazy. They don't know how to act because their ego is in charge.

A person without an ego will not usually be over-reactive. A person without an ego does not have to explain themselves. If I had an ego, I would explain myself and over-explain it.

I would turn it into an escalated emotional event. It's not that you don't have feelings about the situation. You just know yourself and care about yourself better than the situation.

Agent Eph says that you can't be a people pleaser regarding manipulation. You need to make sure how you feel. Be sure of the energy you choose to move above or below you.

Plateeney says: You need to do what you feel. If you were raped psychologically, you have eliminated many things you don't want to consider. If you feel inside, that's why it's good to know, and when you know, you can get rid of the blockages that you don't wanna see. I'm bringing it back to the physic Entity because you have blockages and don't know what they are.

You may need hypnosis or someone who can guide you through releasing some things.

Everyone goes through many things in life, and they say, "Why me? What do I do?" They may question themselves by saying: "Why does no one love me? No one wants to be with me?" All these different issues. But the bottom line is looking at you and seeing the mental problems you need to release or deal with. After your release and dealings with these things, you open up large doorways of who you should be, where you need to move forward, and how to do without this stuff bothering your mind.

Suppose a person has an entity in their mind, and they feed off that woman's energy. They will be attracted to you because they know they can manipulate you even more.

Agent Eph says: I was pretty sharp about this coming from corporate America. At one point, it was a nightmare for some people. I may have had some trust issues. Maybe now it's a blind spot as we are talking, and I wanna fight with you on this. That could be the ego coming out, and I want to say no. I'm not easily manipulated; screw that. I'm a strong woman, and I don't wanna be thought of any other way.

Plateeney says, well, anyone that has to say, "I'm independent." I do my own thing; I make my own money. You have ego problems. As long as you continue to say that, you will probably have relationship problems. Agent Eph says: I Absolutely agree with that.

Plateeney says: So the psychic Entity has to deal with the ego. It also has to deal with the knowledge of curiosity. It goes against what you have been taught your entire life.

Agent Eph says: I just don't wanna be taken advantage of. My parents did their best to teach us not to take shit from anyone.

Plateeney says: That is great, but you can do it without anger. The ego allows a much smaller vibration, putting you in a lower place. It takes practice.

Agent Eph says: It's hard for me to see myself as easily manipulated. I need help to pick up on that.

Plateeney says: I understand. You know the Entity of this. It knows how to manipulate you to get you to be curious enough to keep coming back.

The release aims to get to the point of learning enough knowledge so you don't have to keep coming back. You can do it independently because there has to be a light at the end of the tunnel.

Purgatory was created because they wanted you to go to someone else for knowledge. If the light at the end of the tunnel is always me walking up to you. If you ask what that light needs to look like, I will never get to it, and it will be a more complicated afterlife. It's probably twenty times worse than it needs to be.

You go to somebody who has a lot of issues on their own, yet they are supposed to be able to guide you in the ways of life because they were taught the ways of life by who?

The same people that are controlling them. That's not how we are supposed to learn life.

We are meant to learn life 'within' because God is always connected to us. We do not intend to go looking for God. We are supposed to 'know' that the presence is connected.

It's not a coincidence. And if you think God is not inside. You wouldn't be able to think about that first of all. You wouldn't have the ability to think at all. If you have a brain and a consciousness, God is with you. It's true. You can bring up a lot of different topics related to that.

Many people state that the various faiths have priests, mainly the

Catholic church, spending millions of dollars to cover up a lot of negative child-related situations in Europe. Child cases. (Pauses) So the man you ask to bless your house has negative issues concerning children?

How do you deal with this? What does that do? It makes you turn away from what the energy of God is? You start doubting things. You eventually get to a point where you question everything, and that's why there are problems. This happens because the Entity is there and will never end until you see that God is yourself. Trusting in yourself because there are many beliefs and what is inside, you should have great merit in your consciousness.

Agent Eph says: I think two years ago I went from Catholic church to non-denominational, which I'm learning a lot more things and getting closer to God. What is the Christian belief of what God is, and acquiring as much knowledge as possible going to different avenues of what people would consider "New Age." An example is the law of attraction, even moving into what we are talking about, how people from different galaxies are even more different than what people call the new age.

So now I have a time when you say what is real? You won't know the truth if you keep questioning. You will only know that truth if you go deep within.

Plateeney says: Here is the key. God is who you want it to be when you go within yourself because he is within you to me. It's not debated. It's not because your soul is incarnated into a vessel when you enter the world. You think that's really not of God. Do you think that's not a miracle within itself? Witness one at birth. Think about it for a second. Take the pineal gland in the brain. It causes an electronic process to communicate with your central nervous system. It tells the rest of the body what to do. The central nervous system sends signals for movement and reactions to thinking.

After analyzing that, you will question everything if you believe no God exists. People only question anything about God because there is usually an Entity present. It deals with the same thing. I'm trying to clarify all aspects because believing that you go to a place after you pass on and can't find the light, or what if the light is not natural?

What if or, what if, or what if? You don't ask "what if" when you go within and correctly communicate with the earth and ground. You do what you are told from within. You don't question anything. You don't even have a fear of death. I'm trying to get you to see that the man who did not have an entity on this planet was Jesus Christ, the man they all want to worship and be like. He is the only man that has ever walked on this planet that did not have an entity. He wasn't always so lucky. He looked toward himself, and the more he did, he found love was the key to creating miracles. The more he taught this, the more people wanted to know why he was so full of this high vibration.

Why was he radiating peace and love in the teachings of what he was saying? They wanted to follow him. They didn't want to follow him until they saw him perform a miracle. He performed a miracle not to heal anyone. He didn't need to prove anything to anyone. He did it because he saw a need. But many people only followed or listened once he completed this. This is the biggest problem in the world. It started then.

Agent Eph: I see what you mean. They needed proof.

Plateeney says: People always need evidence in this world. You do not have to prove anything to anyone unless you are selling something and they are asking.

Agent Eph says: The brain is conditioned to have proof.

Plateeney says: It was conditioned because of the controlled system put in place that way. Many years ago, it was put in place.

Agent Eph says: You understand what I am saying about belief and the law of attraction. Basically, your mind asks, "What's the truth?" It may not be any of it. It may be something else. You can make yourself crazy trying to figure that out.

Plateeney states: You can, and eventually, you probably will. When you get aggravated and argumentative, you vibrate a negative feeling and are unhappy. You get drained and all these different words that people use. Here is an example: A vampire believes in what we know as a vampire. A vampire couldn't go in the sun, right? So literally, it would take someone that could go out in the sun, bite them, and feed off the energy of the bloodstream because the bloodstream had Vitamin D. That's what they need to survive. That story is the same thing that I am trying to tell you. The vampire's story is the Entity's actual thought process that sinks its teeth into anyone for you to be manipulated. So when you look at "you," it's not allowed to be managed because you will never allow your gut to be manipulated by someone. It's never going to take place. You always go towards love. The more that love vibrates within you like Jesus.

Exactly like he did, there is no need to be angry, no reason to be argumentative. No need to question. Then you have a mob of people around you who don't like it because it's not their vibration, which is why they crucified him. Because he didn't have to prove to them what he felt. Even though the man with the power said, "no," he knew he shouldn't have allowed Jesus to die. That's karma. The story of Jesus teaches people on the planet what to do and how to stay away from entities. That's what this is.

Agent Eph says: Going back to manipulation, it is making sense. I am always wondering whether I am being manipulated. I need to say there are times when I think, is the preacher manipulative? Is what he saying manipulation? Is all this law of attraction some of the coaching happening possible manipulation trying to get in my head? Some of what we are talking about can be manipulated easily.

Plateeney says: You need to understand something. I know what you are saying, and you need to see this. You don't look within yourself enough because you wouldn't be questioning any of that. You are vulnerable right now because if you Googled all the answers to every question you could have and found someone who could give them to you, you would want to travel to them to find the answers. You would get on a plane and try to find the answers. All the answers are within you. You chose to come back here. Why question you? It is your choice to be here.

Agent Eph says: But even that, you can say, is that true? The brain can wonder about that, too.

Plateeney says The bottom line is you get to a point within yourself when you do not have a vessel. You are no different than a parasite as a soul. The soul parasitically attaches itself to a vessel. (the body) The Entity attaches itself to the body, and it manipulates. Don't think if a woman is battered and has never dealt with that problem. The first thing that will happen is that she will be attracted or the other way around to a person who can and will do the exact same thing to them. It happens all the time. Suppose an entity attaches itself to this woman, any positive person for that woman. In that case, she will run away from it because the vibrations do not match the Entity. Because she is addicted to feeling like shit. And any time someone does something positive for her, she has to create negativity to feel balanced.

Agent Eph: So, she has to traumatize herself to feel normal. I see this a lot with people, and it can be crazy. Plateeney says: But the whole purpose is this: you have been manipulated. Everyone has from the moment that we are born. We are probably managed because if you were raised by someone who was manipulated, you are also being manipulated. You must forgive your parents and grandparents when you go through rehabilitation because they can not teach you these things. It's because they didn't learn it themselves.

Agent Eph says: We may be all manipulated.

Plateeney says: Everyone has been manipulated, and you should want to know why. That is why we should wanna learn from these situations. Here is an example: Anyone can be manipulated. You can go to a foreign country. The first thing that will happen is that any hungry man or woman can manipulate you, especially if they want to. If you are hungry on the street and know you have something, you know. You can make someone feel a sure way to get you something to eat or get something you are hungry for. What's the first thing that you are going to do? You walk up to that person and try to manipulate them. It's up to that person whether or not they wanna feel like they want to help you or not. I get this all the time from individuals. It's almost like an entity. An entity jumps into you and finds your biggest fears and weaknesses. A person walks up to you in the street pregnant and says, My child is starving, and I am too. It's been a while since I ate, and they say I need a bus ticket. What do you do? That is what an entity does to your mind.

Agent Eph says: It makes you question everything about things.

I had someone that asked me at five in the morning. This guy messaged me on my computer and requested me. He looked married. He also looked familiar. His name was familiar, too. I get a message at five in the morning saying, "How are you?" Automatically, I thought this person was trying to flirt with me, so I saw he was local, and I called a mutual friend of ours and asked: "What's with this person?" They told me he was a salesman, and as the conversation continued, we figured out mutually how we may know each other. Then he made a flirtatious comment. Then it went on to what he sells. He then said that someone was a "snake," which immediately turned the conversation sour with his bashing of another company and person.

Plateeney said: But you know that because you know you. So immediately, you should have stopped the conversation because why should you trust the person when he refers to someone as a snake. That immediately indicates that you must stop if you keep going, but here's the deal. If you do keep going, you will just wear yourself out.

Agent Eph says, 'It escalated when I should have just ended the conversation. Yes, it basically did that; it drained me for a while as he tried to follow up and drain me again for a new conversation. And eventually, as it drew negative, I just drew silent, and he continued to ask questions.

Plateeney says: 'He was trying to get a sale by being manipulative, and yes, in the end, it's wasted time and a drained conversation because you knew it was going nowhere, and by going further, you are allowing him to manipulate you.'

Agent Eph says: 'Yes, this is a great example. I usually do not read instructions and say I will put things together. If someone knows this, I would think it could happen.'

Plateeney says, 'People aware of this about you will just wait for you to mess up because you should have followed the instructions in the first place. As an example. Basically, eight out of ten times, you could probably be manipulated.'

Plateeney continued: 'OK, Let's get down to the entity.'

Agent Eph says: 'OK, let's do that.'

The Psychic Entity: I can focus on what your problem is and keep you coming back for more, and the reason is that if I know that you have an issue at work, the more I get to know about you, the more I am going to continue to do it. I am no different than that sales agent because they usually do the same thing. They know your family. They know your families and want you to continue sending them business. It's the exact same thing as a salesman asking for repeat business.

They make a living by continuously knowing more about you and getting you down a spiral because they know it's harder for you to switch the more they know about you. By knowing about you more, manipulation of you happens more. If I know you have a problem speaking, I will force you to talk about things to off-balance your throat chakra. I can off-balance any chakra in your body to make you keep coming back. I can adjust it with the right energy to never make you completely balanced.

Agent Eph says: We all could do that, so no one would ever be better at it than others. But I would feel like an asshole by taking advantage of people.

Plateeney says: That's judgemental.

Agent Eph says: No, I'm saying it's not the right thing to do.

Plateeney says: If you're selling something and make money off it, then in someone else's eyes, depending on what you sold it for. It could be looked at the same way. So you have to think about that.

Agent Eph says: If I am using someone and taking their money and manipulating them like an old couple, that probably has a few bucks.

Plateeney says: But you are getting something. It's a trade-off, so it would seem like there is no karma. There is no pain because you exchange a vow as long as there is an exchange. If you feel like you have something, I can continue to do this because I believe I am doing God's work as an entity, psychic, or anything. But as long as I think that, I can continue to make you believe there is merit and it has volume.

Agent Eph says: Don't you think that's living on the edge?

Plateeney says that very few are pure without greed and ego. Here is an example: That's the ego talking when you say I'm not cool with that.

Agent Eph says: If you are not cool with that, it is ego. I'm not cool with taking advantage of people and greed.

Plateeney says: It doesn't matter if you are cool with it. It's not to stand up and fight with people doing this. What is the learning experience you should take by looking within?

Agent Eph says It's not that; I'm just not cool with it.

Plateeney says: Then how do you get away from it? I understand it's challenging to comprehend. The reason you feel the way you feel states that you have an ego to release.

Agent Eph says: I do know on some level.

Plateeney says: If you told me that you manipulated me because you slowly but steadily knew me, I would say OK, have a good day, and I would walk away, and I would never return. I would always look within from that point on and send you peace. Agent Eph says: I am in agreement with that.

Plateeney says: But you don't say I feel sorry for it. Any plan or intent you are thinking about someone else. As long as there is the intent, there is a reaction to what you call the law of attraction. You are attracting it by saying it aloud. You immediately feel at peace if you don't say or think anything. You can surround yourself with love and the other person and walk away.

You can say: "Now I know I only need to look within and send myself peace." At that point, you don't need guidance. You have control of yourself. You can see for yourself. You can communicate with God through yourself. You can radiate love. As much as you radiate love, there won't be entities surrounding you.

There will be no entities when you live in the radiation and vibration of love. Entities don't resonate with this. This is why you don't see Buddhist monks hanging out in a bar; they don't need to.

They are perfectly OK with being themselves and by themselves. This is why the Kung Fu Master does not need to fight. He would rather not have a confrontation.

It makes you curious to know what it was because, at that moment, you realize there is a God. A Master would rather take a punch than have a fight. He may also be a master of Chi energy. This can push you away and make you understand that energy pushes you through the hands.

This energy (Chi) is created by having so much energy within yourself that you can create an element that is how strong you can be as a human. You can create elemental manifestations. You can create fire. You can create. You can create all these things. You are water; the majority of your body is water already. You breathe the air; you are all one with the elements. If you feel those elements daily, no part of your body will be of God. You will always understand that your body is an element. It's not a physical thing like we believe.

It's a matter of the elements. The desire to want to love is fire. You are finding elements within yourself and your own mind through your soul. This is the lesson of looking within yourself. Does this make sense?

Because if you had no water, you wouldn't be able to survive. Your organs would shut down, and you would die. The elements are God. You would cease to exist if you couldn't stand on the earth. You couldn't ground the magnetism properly and would not allow the brain to persist incorrectly. It's different. So what now?

Agent Eph says: What are your techniques for people to get centered. I know meditation.

Plateeney says: Grounding is always first. You only ever do something with grounding. You put your feet on the earth, and if you don't put your feet physically on the ground, visualize it happening through the base of your spine as an exercise. I recommend closing your eyes and focusing on roots from the spine's base down to the earth. This also goes through the feet and into the soil of the earth.

You are touching land, and what happens is you are just visualizing your body's movement. You then imagine the roots within your body in the base of your spine, moving through the soil the same way you would plant in the garden. When you do this, your body balances itself. Your spine adjusts itself. The spine communicating with the earth perfectly understands that your body must interact with that element to be balanced. Does this make sense?

How do you feel right now?

Agent Eph says: I'm relaxed but have a little anxiety in my chest.

Plateeney says: It's because you need to release some energy. You have blockages that are trying to come out. You just don't think you do.

Agent Eph says: I have something in my chest right now. It feels like a heavy feeling.

Plateeney says: Ask to release it. This is precisely what I mean for you to understand that you must ground. Grounding will allow your body to go back to the earth. Your body can only hold on to so much energy, which becomes balanced when you ground the energy transfer. This is how chakra balance takes place unless someone does it for you. You could be way out of sync.

This is where a Reiki master can help you balance your chakra system. It's only to get rid of the trauma. Because we have a lot of it on each of us. Everyone goes through trauma. If you drink alcohol, have blacked out, and forgotten who you were, that's trauma. Imagine the traumas you forget subconsciously. You can't release one without a ritual of physical output. You can eventually, but releasing will be much more harmful to you. This is why looking within yourself allows you to move forward. You can immediately feel that you have a problem with your chest.

The right way to do this is not "Hey, psychic, what's bothering me in my chest?"

Agent Eph says: OK, Psychic Entity, what is bothering me in my chest?

Plateeney says it's emotions from a previous relationship, not just one but two. You can set an intention and release them one by one with that knowledge. The more you do this, and the more you release these things, you will see by grounding when they are not there anymore, and then you know you took care of the problem. But here is the deal: by grounding and understanding, there is a problem when you ask. It is not because you want to win the lottery or not because you want to have sex with a co-worker. Does this make sense?

That's how you stay within yourself, and the funniest, most fantastic thing about it is understanding that intuitiveness exists. It's the first part of your release. When you release, you realize you don't need intuitive people anymore because you become intuitive. You activate yourself within yourself.

You become a part of God… and that's it.

Entity 5

THE OBSESSION ENTITY

Plateeney and Agent Eph are in a room, and we must leave. We are being told to take a break because we must exit our location for some reason and then return later. We are being ordered to do so. We are in New York, and it's cold and snowing. We will explain how we can get to these dimensions and interview and conversate with these things (entities).

Plateeney and Agent Eph are part of an underground agency. It's a mixture of National and Galactic forces in one. There is a symbol on each of them, but there is no name, just a device allowing access to hidden areas. It is hard to pinpoint the level of secrecy.

You can call it foreign nations or something of another world. The logo is a circle, but they don't wear the symbol like regular law enforcement. It is embedded in their DNA. It is not crucial to the pair, but it should be addressed that it is a part of their consciousness. It is a feeling of ownership. The team is supposed to be clothed similarly to what one would know on Earth as the FBI. It's just (Plateeney), and he is walking to meet Agent Eph.

Plateeney looks about sixty feet ahead. He can see Agent Eph is waiting for him to arrive in a large modern lobby area as they attempt to enter the next facility. They are not allowed to approach the compound separately.

Agent Eph meets up with Plateeney, and they are now about to contact each other. Plateeney walks down and approaches an elevator. They both proceed to a hallway with a lot of glass in the building's front. As Plateeney looks around visually, he can see a vast area of the building they are inside now. He thinks to himself that it actually looks like a hotel. We continue walking down a large hallway with nothing on the floor. "Our lives are interesting," states Agent Eph as they approach the hall. She continues: "We don't worry about money. We can basically do whatever we want. We can say what we want, but we can also speak to each other telepathically to steal our minds from others around us. It's almost like we are not entirely human, but we have some "press pass" to go anywhere we want, like a crime scene. (anything) We don't have jurisdictional issues. We have full clearance ultimately."

{For example, the FBI cannot follow them into many clearance rooms because they cannot pursue. It is unknown to humans that the pair's most significant thing is not authorized to associate with other humans. That's the one thing that seems weird about this situation. They are trained not to have emotion towards the people around them. The things that we come in contact with daily are just there. The pair still look human, but they must remember that they are only visually human because people don't relate to them the same way. It's almost like you are the FBI. No one speaks to you, so it's OK, and mainly, if you don't verbalize when spoken to, people just deal with it.}

Agent Eph continues: "Others know that if we don't talk because of our training, we must be of a higher classification and clearance. They are also trained not to proceed in thought with us because it may be fatal for them. There is virtually something different about us, Plateeney. We have another symbol on our badges, so we immediately bring a presence many know not to bombard if we are present. We are not usually present unless a situation calls for a higher clearance. We don't often have issues with a healthy attachment to humans."

Plateeney sent a transmission to Agent Eph: "I saw myself in a previous relationship in a dream last. I downloaded an explanation about the way this entity works and its control. It showed me a visual of what happens with this entity inside of a relationship. Then, it showed me an example of why we can't date at all in this world. We are not allowed to have relationships anymore. We are not human. If you have a soul, you are not human. The vessel is the human, and you take it on. When you die, your soul moves forward to something else. The term "human" was created because people need a reason to be OK. One example is, "You are only human." It's an excuse. OK, we are in a body and have a soul connected to something unrelated to the human body. You are still your soul, but the soul controls the human body, similar to how a finger can hold a standard television remote control. It is not positive for us to have emotions for another human because almost every human has an entity. Nearly 20% or less of the human population has no entity."

"We can feel love and understand what it is. Still, there is no constant touch, marriage, or relationship. One of the reasons why priests and nuns are not allowed to marry is that we can only move forward differently. Co-mingling with humans is the reason behind it. Not all are of this stature, but it's the mindset behind it. This example is similar to a program or ritual that must be considered seriously. You might as well be human, have a life, and show people truthful examples similar to God. There is no reason to be different and dress differently. You are just practicing a life of ritual that programs others. And the others are programmed to follow you because you are a follower of the highest. (Messiah) The Messiah is usually portrayed as not being human. Which is the underlying factor behind this situation?"

Agent Eph looks at Plateeney and slowly fades her left eye, thinking to herself. "That is some dream download, you know." Plateeney smiles sideways as the two meet at the lobby entrance and approach a black car. Plateeney raises his wrist near the door, and the vehicle runs.

Agent Eph approaches the passenger side, and the two enter this black vehicle. The vehicle shows them a map and slowly comes to a building. The building is a warehouse-style garage similar to a military facility. The building map shows the pair a display on the vehicle's windshield as it self-drives.

The car moves slowly and then drives straight through a brick wall. The wall becomes liquefied as all move directly through it, and the feeling is fast to the pair but precisely like walking through a wall of water. (teleportation) As the team approaches the other side of the wall, the car stops near an entrance. The wall behind them has sealed rather quickly again, and they are then surrounded by cinder blocks with no way out.

There are two men with semi-automatic machine gun rifles at two separate entrances. Plateeney and Agent Eph move towards a door and walk through the doors the same liquefied way the car drove through the wall earlier. The pair step out of the vehicle after the doors pop open.

Agent Eph and Plateeney go through a checkpoint on the other side, receive a folder, and then step into an elevator at the end of a dark hallway. As the two approach the elevator, the temperature gets cooler, about 67 degrees. As the doors close, they become liquefied on the elevator, and they start to have a wave-like pattern on all four corners as the doors close.

The two stand in the center, and the doors start to move in and out faster, becoming a wave-like formation. As these walls move, the pair becomes a part of the dimension they are objected to.

{The dimension name is unimportant, but what is known is that we are now in the same dimension as the entities. Our mission is to interrogate them more for personal training and research while in the field for part of the job we have.}

{Plateeney and Agent Eph are learning more about them because they are also a part of life on Earth. They will encounter them daily in most others dealing with regular human life. They also need to figure out what they may be dealing with in humans heavily saturated with these entities.}

One objective for the pair is to figure out how to stop the natural programming through TV media and all different outlets so quickly that people do not commit suicide.

Humanity can't deal with its decompression of it. Society cannot process rapid frequency changes such as these. No one wants to end life on the planet, but taking the proper steps to be strategic is vital. The organization behind this operation is different from the actual Planet Earth owners. They have to be careful when making the right decisions.

Other species on Earth allow some of these things to occur. Here is the real story because we are in training. We are also not fully human, but you would perceive some Galactic agency or government police. We are here to allow and learn how to interact with these entities to not manipulate us at higher levels. We can hear things more in-depth; we do not need excellent eyesight; we need great insight, so we need to feel the energy from someone to sense if they are living. Instead of having two lungs, we have one, so we breathe differently than a regular human. We don't really think with our eyes. Our voices are there because we are sometimes forced to communicate with others; otherwise, we would not speak at all. We use natural telepathy daily to communicate with each other. I will also include that we wear dark clothing, but we are not wearing black. We wear dark, deep navy blue, black shoes, and darker accents to blend in as a natural agent.

Still, our weapons are also very unlike traditional federal agencies. These entities think we can't get rid of them. They have the upper hand. After all, they know we can't get rid of something we can't see with the eye because they are not in this dimension. They are unhappy and nervous when we are in their dimension because they know we can see them (which they do not like). They do not like feeling vulnerable, yet they make humans feel like that daily. It's cowardly because when the shoe is on the other foot, they have difficulty dealing with it entirely. We return to the original room with yellowish-colored walls as we get where we need to go. We walk through the hallway, and it's like a weird cubicle-filled room but larger-sized cubicles.

None of these entities are happy that they are being contained. They are also not delighted to be questioned. As we walk up to the Obsession entity, we can see it's a female, but I must clarify that it can take shape. If the entity feels the need, it can assume a man's body. It's the mindset that is what we are dealing with. At this time, I see a female with royal blue hair and a white-skinned body. (Think toothpaste tube white) We giggle for a second as we realize she is right before us to get acquainted.

The entity is aware that we are viewing her in front of a piece of glass and does not like that we can see her or any form of her whatsoever.

Her pupils are red as she looks up at us, but the rest of her eyes are white, similar to humans. She locks on you when you are in front of her like a robot, viewing you as a target. She looks non-human, but you can tell she is very warrior-like if she needs to be.

Agent Eph is very anxious to speak to her. She asks the entity if she has a name.

Plateeney says out loud, "Crazy?" When he expresses this, the entity locks on him and stares at Plateeney, wanting to reach out to him, but she knows she cannot.

You can tell the judgment is not something she is interested in. She does not want to speak, and she does not like us. She knows she is being forced to, so she is cooperating.

Agent Eph states another question again. Do you have a favorite obsession?

The obsession entity, once again, does not understand the question asked. The entity reports having no idea what an obsession is. Entities continue to explain that the term needs to be understood or is part of their programming.

Plateeney explains that she knows her objective, and that is all. Her job is what she knows and how to survive to move forward. Anything having to do with what she is a part of, she does not understand because it is a part of her objective to survive. If the entity understood all that she did, she would be human. This is not at all the case because she uses humanity to feed. She will never admit she is a problem.

Agent Eph is confused about how to proceed. Plateeney states that she needs to interrogate her like cross-referencing a human in the court system. It's like you are trying to confuse a person similar to court because they won't admit to doing anything wrong, so you must re-word your question, like, Did you enjoy Thanksgiving? Or would you enjoy a celebration called Thanksgiving?

This questioning method is used to learn from the obsession entity because they only show themselves when an obsession is near. OK, let me try again.

Agent Eph states: Do you like to gamble? The entity says that she does not like to do anything at all. I just do what I am programmed to do by the humans I am attached to.

Have you ever gambled? Asked Agent Eph?

The entity says: I do not know what gambling is. This continues with the questions: Have you ever been to a casino? Have you ever enjoyed card games?

Plateeney steps in and asks: Where did you go last night? The entity changes her look of confusion, smiles, and says I felt myself move through a body with two other entities. The other entities present were Alcohol and Sexual Entities. I sit, wait, and watch the two other entities every night because they show me when to do my job. It's like I am their adrenaline in some way. So, as they overpower a human (soul disconnect), they may look towards me as extra energy. It's like they are looking towards me to add extra energetic resources to disconnect a person from their soul to continue manipulating on an extreme level.

This is stronger when I am dormant; they know I am also there. We all work together for typical output. The various entities know their job, and I know mine. I just sit back, waiting. I just wait patiently.

Agent Eph says,: Then what do you do?

The entity status: I wait until they ask me for more energy.

Agent Eph asks: What does this mean?

The entity explains: It's like I am breathing or blowing on something like the wind blows like a tornado.

Agent Eph says: What does this energy do to a human? It makes them not see things clearly. It's like an adrenaline rush that won't allow them to see straight. An example is when someone says, "I can't see straight; I was so angry." This is one factor of how you know we are present. We can input patterns and thoughts to the subconscious to implement a more destructive behavioral pattern in a human.

Agent Eph says: How does a person become obsessed?

The entity explains: They slowly become obsessed with other entities first. I may not be there for a while, actually. The other entities get them angry or fueled up. The more control they have over the host, the better.

Agent Eph asks: Can you do this without the other entities?

I can, but it is complicated to accomplish.

Agent Eph asks again: So you are an entity that likes to work with other entities?

One example is that people may say I was so angry that I saw red. The entity rolls her eyes and explains: No, we don't like to, but I usually have to. This is our mechanism to block your typical reaction pattern to do what we are sending frequencies to accomplish to your consciousness.

Agent Eph: So, do you have the ability to make a human angry at all?

The entity quickly says: Yes, but it is tough to do by myself. The other entities present don't exactly like that I am there. It gives them extra power, and they love power, so they are OK with it once they see it. It makes them feel more in control. Their feeling is very similar to nitrous oxide in a race car. The car is the vessel (human), and the driver is the entity. Nitrous oxide is the obsession entity. This may be the best way to understand this process. Does this make sense?

I and the other entities energetically 'hold hands' to disallow connection to your soul. I allow the others to take the entire body over once we are matched equally. We take a thought and ensure its entity is driven once it is...

Agent Eph says: Is it easy to influence once you get disconnected from the soul? The entity states that caffeine is the substance used to start manipulating. When a human drinks caffeine, the body feels like it's amplified, making it possible to move things around, but when it gets too much of something, it gets tired and goes to sleep. Your body needs rest to heal, and if, for some reason, the sleep routine becomes changed, we can use the change chemically to make it work for us slowly by working with the energies. Before you sleep under any influence, you can enter your dream state before entering a state of healing. If we do this, we can make you deteriorate. If you have problems sleeping, it's not because you have insomnia. Because you are under some influence, there is an entity present. They are slowly doing their job to unbalance you. You have to perform the ritual of sleep to heal correctly.

It's part of your daily basis and part of your routine. You must remember you need to rest, which is why routine sleep is essential. When you get off this balance of sleep routine, it makes you vulnerable, and it's easier for us to take you over. Caffeine is the easiest thing because some humans touch caffeine in the bloodstream for the first time at around five years of age. Cigarettes are another one. The ritual of you smoking, the hands moving back and forth (you say it's calming.) The entity laughs and states: We don't understand how humans think it's calming. It adds a strain and uses an electro-shock treatment to the bloodstream and the body. We love people who smoke, and if you do drugs, there is nothing we cannot do. Agent Eph says: Is the internet an obsession to get humans to move away from their focus? The entity says: I don't understand.

Agent Eph says: Persuading someone to become addicted or obsessed with something, how do you do this? Like video game addiction or drugs? The entity grows tempered and says: We won't convince anyone to do anything. Once you are hooked, then we move in slowly. A person goes to the internet because of another entity; it's not because of me.

Agent Eph says: What is an obsession you can pull off without other entities even though it's hard? The entity says: Slowly, slowly, being around the opposite sex. We are not a sexual entity. But we can slightly move the thoughts by swaying them to think about someone more than expected. When you hear the Ego say, I want to buy a new house, your reasoning behind the idea is 65% because your friends have one. Then you can be assured that we have something to do with this.

Agent Eph says: So you can use the Ego to drive an obsession.

The entity happily says: Yes, we can. We have to wait 45 days for us to give you impulses. The more Ego you have, the more you will be present, but here is the thing: a regular addiction takes twenty-one days.

Agent Eph says: As you become more connected to the Ego and less attached to the soul, the obsession will step in and take over more frequently.

The entity says: Anything that makes you feel like you must feel and do better than someone else...is an obsession. Anything that drives you outside the typical spectrum of who you are is an obsession. Anything that makes you stop thinking about your life's happiness is an obsession. Anything that makes you feel like you are not yourself is an obsession. Anything that makes you do things that feel like they are not you. If you have to sleep with married men. If you have to find a woman to fuck. I say that, but if you find any random person and feel you must screw that person, that's an obsession. It's the start of the addiction.

Agent Eph says: Is alcohol an obsession?

The entity says: No, it's a straight-up addiction.

Agent Eph says: Do positive obsessions exist? The entity leans back in her chair and says: No.

Agent Eph says: Are there any obsessions that are not ego-driven? The entity once again says NO.

Agent Eph asks: What's the most dangerous obsession? The entity sits in silence for a while and says, equal, they are all equal. We all operate at the same pulse. We don't try to go faster or slower; we are just one straight pulse shot, so no matter your objective, it feels completely normal.

Agent Ephs states: You have no control, and I believe that's true. Here is an example of why it's easier. I understand the obsession, but the closer I get to the source, I have the most control over the right direction. The entity says: You have all control when you're connected to your soul. But we can easily disconnect you from the soul if you have an ego. So when people have an ego, they think they are in control the most, which can be ironic. But truthfully, the most possible time they are not in control is when they are full of Ego. The Ego makes you highly vulnerable as a human. In its own regard, the Ego is similar to an entity even though it's not.

Agent Eph says: How hard is it to break an obsession?

The entity says it takes the same time for someone to break an addiction as it is to break an obsession. But the obsession still hangs out for at least sixty days, so we remain lingering. Once you forget, the obsession sits dormant, and you have to ask a direct higher power to take it from you, and after it happens quite a bit, then possibly yes.

Agent Eph asks: Is there an obsession that we should be discussing that we are unaware of?

The entity says: Not at this time. No. Agent Eph asks: What is something you want to tell us?

The entity says: "I don't need to tell you anything."

Agent Eph says: The others didn't want to tell us anything. But you have to do so. That's why we are here.

The entity says The best way to explain it is how a car works. The car is there, the nitrous bottles are in the back, and the engine or driver is the entity. The car cannot function without fuel, making it move. The engine is like the brain. You put a different kind of gas, which becomes an entity that makes you feel better and different, like a drug, caffeine, or nicotine. At that point, you may be able to decipher where you want to go, but the more you continue to take on drugs and all the entities. Here is the deal: you may take on one drug one day and think you have it handled because you don't bring them daily.

Then you may get a different drug, like the same kind of drug, but slightly different, and it may mess your complete equilibrium off balance.

Your brain may think that you have it covered for thirty days, but here is one that is a little more aggressive, and you may have one that is not as aggressive and still waits as an entity, so this is kind of how it gets you to think you need more than one pill to work.

Once you get more than one, you have the entity. You have an entity once you take a second pill because your mindset thinks one does not work. Because one actually does work, it's just the entity making you believe that it's not. When you take another one, the obsession is being asked for me to intervene by the entity.

Example: I took one pill, which did not work, so I took a second. OK, now it works. I feel it. When you think this, it's the entity setting up the brain for an obsession.

Once an obsession becomes dormant, I can control the entity. And that's what I don't want to say. We can a computer program the entity at that point. The entity can do whatever it wants until it chooses the obsession to take it over. So, say you're interested in a man, and we know what he will want from you. We allow you to open up certain inhibitions, especially under the influence. So when you start opening up these inhibitions, we know how to take you over and how you work, so we know it has to be a process for the obsession to fully take you over. We are aware it will take time (sometimes it does). It just depends on the situation you were in previously. You don't communicate with humans because you never know where someone was before. You have to learn this process once attached. So humans have terms for everything that happens, so they genuinely believe they are fine. So when they are not OK, they continue to explain that they are not slow.

Indeed, humans return to the same routine, which makes them escape the fact that they had a problem before. They believe that they are fine, which makes them more vulnerable. We know it makes you more vulnerable when we get you away from this thinking. It's one of the ways that we make you more vulnerable to wanna take something on. Because this is where sleep deprivation comes in and many others. You can become obsessed with the fact that you don't sleep. You can also become obsessed with the fact that you sleep too much. You have an entity if you take sleeping pills because you think you can't sleep. Suppose you think you can't do something. In that case, you immediately resort to going on to something else, a chemical you are obsessed with. At this point, you are obsessed. When you are not in control, you are obsessed.

Agent Eph asks: Is there an attention obsession? Do you know people who do things for attention?

Attention is an obsession if you put something online strictly because you want to feel something you are obsessed with. You should never make someone you open yourself for an entity attachment. The entity states:

That's the number one way we regularly program the brain. Entities eat this stuff up. They wait for it to be what they crave. That's why we don't control the sexual entity. Once it's under our control, we have to allow the sexual entity to do its job, and when we send signals to make it stronger, we take it over. It's all a quest for power, but we still need to allow it to do its job. It's like riding a bike, but I have five other people pedaling. Like the captain of a boat, but there are seven engines.

I can have seven entities, but I may be driving the wheel no matter what. The second I take my hand off the wheel, an entity starts driving my body. It doesn't matter what it is. It could be from the internet to driving faster, eating something, and craving. If you consider yourself to crave something, you have a parasitic entity.

You are not only close to obsession, but you are also coming in and out of it. You do this because we are trying to make you more and more vulnerable so you can take more control.

We detach you from your soul while taking on as many entities as possible.

Agent Eph asks: What about an eating obsession?

The entity says: The eating obsession is... I am not ever going to admit that things are an obsession. You need to understand that I'm not programmed like that.

I'm not going to want people to believe there is an issue. Eating is something that you enjoy; Overeating is an Obsession Entity. One that has to have the same drug. For many people, food is a drug. It's probably more of an addiction that can slowly become an obsession.

Agent Eph asks: What about having to eat out all the time?

The entity says: This is not an obsession if you feel like you must always eat out. You are just eating to fuel your body. It's not considered to be an obsession. I don't have an entity I wait for that will hand it off to me, making it an obsession. The more you don't feel good, the more you do not exactly help us. We want you to feel like you are in tip-top shape, and when you don't, it's because another entity is feeding off of the energy you have.

Agent Eph asks: You were speaking about online posts and how you should not do it for a reaction or a response. Do you remember that?

The entity says: I'm saying you don't want to write something if all you need is extreme gratification. That would slowly become an obsession, and it all becomes an obsession if all you do is wait for gratification. That would still not become a complete obsession because our ultimate goal is to get you to react. Humans call it when we get you to respond in anger or a crazy state like you. That's a complete obsession. It would be an obsession if you couldn't do anything that day without writing something for gratification. Brushing your teeth fifteen times a day is an obsession.

If you have to be careful not to walk on the cracks in the sidewalk, that is an obsession. That will be an obsession if you masturbate fifteen times daily just to feel good. And all these things. Having to feel good is not an obsession because it gives you feel good if it's done out of love. This is because it raises the vibration. If it's done out of anger, then it's an obsession. Can you love it too much? Yes, which could possibly become an obsession.

Agent Eph: What if you are obsessed with a person?

The entity explains that you are obsessed if you love someone too much. If there is a problem with loving too much, it's an obsession.

Agent Eph: Are you sure?

The entity says: Yes, let me explain: you can send someone mental love through telepathic reasons. It's like a prayer. But when you love someone too much, it's like rubbing a stuffed bear and rubbing it too frequently that you rub the hair off of the bear. It starts with a feeling that you want to be connected, and then that person shows you the connection. Still, that person's entity is working with the other entity. It's not co-dependent. You see something within that person that makes you connected to that person. This is just proof that this person has an entity. Because it knows how to think about what you want. It knows what you want in time, especially after knowing you for a short period, and does this because it lacks dependency.

Agent Eph says: It does this when someone is needy.

The entity explains: That's not an entity that someone who feels the extreme need in they feel like doing. It's more of an obsessive compulsion, not a strict obsession. If a person texts you all day, repeatedly, it depends on what kind of entities they have. Still, it's almost like entities will not allow it to deal with a previous issue when that happens. Like something is trying to remove itself. It keeps reminding the other person about a previous situation that it has not dealt with. That's how you get these things. But it's not an obsession. Let me explain. When we do our work, we are masters of what we do. We are programmed for it. You are programmed to live. We are programmed to live off of you.

So, as much as you are driven to live, we are just as driven to be programmed to live off you. Figuring out every detail and angle we love the most makes you feel you need to know everything. That's the worst thing that you can do. You want to learn everything, and it lets us know that you will allow us in. You allow yourself to become addicted, and it's your choice. If you want to know what it feels like on the other side. There is always such curiosity among these humans. You just want to know. You always want to know, and that can become an obsession. Too much interest can become an obsession that I don't even control.

That's an obsession that God controls, but I know it will help me, so I allow myself to wait because that is not something I need to waste my time on. The fact that you get curious and want to learn is just my way of saying thank you, God. Your curiosities and learning capabilities allow me to make you even more interested. And when an entity is inside of you, it will make you more vulnerable. When you are vulnerable, you can become obsessed regularly. So, how do you not become weak?

Agent Eph says: You must be secure and confident in who you are.

The entity says: The answer is ultimate inner peace and self-acceptance on all levels. If you have self-acceptance, look at yourself in the mirror and forget the vessel you are inside and how it physically looks like you are close. When you stop thinking about other people's appearance or how they feel about you. Then, you can completely destroy all entities and obsessions. If you do that, we will no longer exist. And it deals with complete self-contentment if you can look at yourself in the mirror and not even say I love you.

At that point, you just know there is love and vibrate love for yourself, and that's OK. We have no control, even if you're congested. But it takes extreme discipline to open your mind to thinking an entity is controlling you. When you open your mind to this, we immediately set up mechanisms to somehow deal with this in your mindset. Then, it takes 24 hours to process this in the brain itself. So, depending on how you deal with it, we either move closer after the first 24 hours or die.

If you sit down, you have inner peace because you might not have been the cause of your divorce, your children not have the ability to be in your life, or you killed five people because you decided to drive intoxicated.

Then you start to understand that this is not who you are, and when you realize this and see it's not your fault, you can forgive yourself and go back to acceptance. You go back to square one. So, when you are obsessed, you are driving yourself to the form of obsession. You have to drive faster to fulfill your obsession if you drive fast. And if you drive slowly, then it happens slowly. Who has that obsession? It's all about going faster and better than more. When you consistently fulfill all these thoughts, you become more easily controlled. But it's still, once again, your choice.

So, suppose you allow the entity to think for you or enable the obsession to think of the entity. In that case, we can put more of a wall around your body to disconnect you from the soul.

Believe it or not, when people are in rehab and detoxing, sometimes you will hear someone speak in another voice or tone, and people say that's a demon. We think it is funny because we don't know what a demon is. We laugh at this. We don't know what a demon is at all. This makes keeping you under the influence even easier because you believe something is taking you over. But it's not even a thing. We are like a frequency program. If you suspect a demon exists, that's just putting more control on yourself. You can completely control the fact that something is there. I mean, have you ever seen a demon? Why would you believe it exists? It's just programming. This whole purpose of having to believe can also become an addiction. And once that habit becomes active, it can become the worst obsession ever.

And that's where you have some problems with that because some of the things people have made others believe for the last century are that people shouldn't believe or shouldn't be any belief.

You should worship this and all the various things you have thrown at you daily. I think the same way you can become addicted and obsessed with the fact that you have to think a lot to believe. I believe that is an obsession that's as close to giving us the ability to do everything we do. So, how do you survive with all these various things around you? And that's the part where I tell you you must try. And if you can't, you are making it susceptible to you. But once an entity makes its home in your body and says you go to a store, you have to smoke weed that night and do it. Then you return to a random store and have to smoke weed again.

Then you do it again, and then once every blue moon, the fact that made you believe that you had to do it again is a slow entity to make you feel that you just didn't feel terrible that day because I did that.

OK, and this is going to be a difficult situation to explain. You can never feel bad. You are just creating something to make it easier for your thoughts. It's not the fault of a person because they were raped. Still, if you walk into a place infested with entities just because you are different. They know you have something they want to feel good about, so you put yourself in an entity-driven situation.

If it makes you happy to get that gratification, you are obsessed and putting yourself in harm's way. It's not your fault if someone reacts. But you must understand and know that other people have thoughts about you. You should feel those thoughts when you walk into a room with nothing but entities. You should have that ability. Some people actually enjoy and welcome it. The chances of you having the same entity as the "rapist" are pretty good, and if that's the case, then you probably both share the same. I am saying that an entity will take advantage of a woman. (or the opposite)

There is an entity obsession with a man that will rape a woman because an entity feeds off of your fear. (or the opposite again) He keeps asking for more energy to take you over physically. It's not his body that can get you over. The strength and boost of the obsession that allows that man to become someone else is the same thing that allows the entity to take on the complete form of another person's body. So basically, if a person is so addicted to a substance that they are lying on the street and someone walks past them, they get up to hurt another person walking past them. The person that reacts to damage the other still goes to jail to reap the problems of what the entity did to them.

So basically, it's up to you to figure it out because I would almost be willing to bet that over 35% of the people incarcerated today will tell you they don't even remember what happened.

Agent Eph asks: What can we do to stay away from an entity, mainly to avoid it, or what should we look out for?

The entity says: You really can't do anything.

Agent Eph asks: We are helpless?

You will beat entities until a person figures out what we are trying to determine is how you make. The entity says: That's what I want you to believe, but you must remember that you already have an entity if I am involved. We have already made you co-dependent to make you need us.

Agent Eph: How do we avoid the obsession entity?

The entity says: If you have an obsession, it's because you have an entity. But you are not listening to me. What I mean is what we are working on now the same way some humans believe scientists are working on a cure for cancer? They are not. There will not be a cure for anything. The only difference is that you will have an obsession with the need for an entity. That is currently what they are working on now. A deeper intrusion into you. Do you believe they don't know about this for a second? All addiction and your entity drive are so good because, basically, many doctors are the ones pushing it. They are the entity drug dealer; it's not only Ego driving. It's what they are programmed to do.

It's simple when you work eighty hours a week in the emergency room, with no pay for some time, and start wanting to heal the world.

Then you see the world is infested with entity-driven gangs shooting each other daily and nightly drugs and dealers killing each other daily with no care for life itself?

Then you realize that people function like this daily, and you are on the front line most of the time. You may try to help, and you see the same people consistently with the same re-occurring issues weekly. You see gunshots every day and thousands of addictions. This can eventually make you say... "Well, I might as well make some money off this too." People will arrive and fake an illness to get a prescription for anything to fill the need for addiction. It's almost like, who's to say maybe they will hurt themselves and stop asking one day. We have to think about that for a second. What would you do if you constantly have someone who asks you for a dollar, and then they ask you for a 5-dollar bill one day?

Would you just keep on giving them the dollars and fives? Or would you make them go away? How do you get them to go away? Think about that for a second. Does this make sense? You continue hurting yourself, especially when you don't care to help yourself because you are so congested with entities. The purpose of being called a controlled substance is to tell you that you have an entity?

Another example would be the spirits in a liquor store. Why walk into that liquor store if you thought a ghost was in your drink and were scared of a haunted house? If you are scared of a ghost being in your drink, why open the door to the haunted house, especially if you are afraid of haunted houses.

Humans are not the sharpest tools in the shed. It makes sense. If you knew that your boyfriend was doing this daily... drinking haunted houses, and you were scared of them, would you want to be around your boyfriend?

Agent Eph says: No, of course not.

The entity: This is why we sit around and telepathically say to ourselves: "These fucking people are crazy." The obsession entity laughs while Agent Eph looks around and looks worn out. What's sad is when you start judging people like this, too. Judgment can also have the ability to make you vulnerable, so it keeps going on and on and on. The more paranoid you get, the better you get. Then you judge the people around you, and we can still infiltrate this situation. Do you understand?

Agent Eph says: "Yes, I do. I don't think we need to go further."

Plateeney says after seeing Agent Eph look very tired. "Let's Go."

Entity 6

THE WHISPER & THE CHANNEL

Today, Plateeney & Agent Eph are getting information from the Obsession entity. The pair make eye contact and take a step back, then immediately are guided by two armed guards who walk them down the hall and out of the tan cubicle-filled rooms.

Plateeney & Agent Eph slowly walk down a colder hallway and enter another complex with dark walls. It looks more like a modern hotel with empty walls. Very clean again, but dark. We approach a doorway and see padded walls in a large room with two beings inside. As the pair approach the room inside, they realize less containment is present, just padded black walls.

Agent Eph and Plateeney look at each other, asking where the containment surrounding is? The two beings are chained inside the room, but no outside containment exists. They are threatening because we know they are in this room, but the agents know they must be more alert to the surroundings. The agents have yet to learn who they are or what's happening.

Plateeney & Agent Eph also need to figure out what will happen. The two beings are entirely silent and without movement. Agent Eph never moves his eyes when he approaches the male looking up at her.

The male coldly stares but does not move his eyes, which is startling. The agents walk in with chairs inside the room a bit further after someone brings them inside so they can sit down.

The Entity stares at Agent Eph again as Plateeney watches him closely.

Plateeney realizes the female is chained to this Entity and starts staring closer at Agent Eph as I approach. Still, they both just stare at Agent Eph, and I get a little frazzled at them both, staring like she is a steak, so I get ready for just about anything at this time and wait just before I sit down.

Plateeney knows if she moves for some reason, he will approach her for Agent Eph and his safety. They are both extraordinarily entity-driven and out of their minds from an intuitive feeling.

Agent Eph looks at Plateeney and wonders what I am thinking.

Agent Eph asks, "Do they have instructions not to approach us?"

Plateeney says, "We should have been briefed, but let's see where this goes.

Agent Eph and Plateeney make eye contact in the room, then move toward each other slowly while reaching for their chairs.

The two know they are going into this Entity situation on their own. It's also two Entities simultaneously, which is riskier, but they are aware of the consequences.

Plateeney looks at Agent Eph and asks, "Do you want to start?

Agent Eph says, "You go first."

Plateeney looks at them and asks, Why are you two together?

The male figure states: "Well, we actually work together." (After looking around the room very amused)

The female entity stays still and silent while staring at Agent Eph. She is trying to intimidate her a bit mentally. Agent Eph continues to look at her notebook. She keeps one eye on the female entity because we are experiencing some strange activity from the girl since we have now started to speak to them.

As impressive as the entire interrogation process has been, the pair do not know what is expected of these two in the room. Still, Plateeney and Agent Eph didn't figure it could be stranger than previously.

Plateeney asks again: "OK, so you work together; what does that mean?"

The male entity claims that he is a channel frequency. And whenever the agents talk to her, she does not stop staring at Agent Eph.

Plateeney asks the male entity if he can speak on behalf of her? "Is this possible?"

And he says: "Yes, I can do that?"

Agent Eph asks him If the female Entity can talk?

The male Entity states, "She cannot do this at this time, but yes, she will speak, just not right now when she feels the need. Neither one of us wants to be here. We were asked to be here for a reason."

Plateeney says: "So you are a channeler, but what about her? What does she do?

The Channel Entity says: "She is an entity that allows me to do my work," he states.

"Which is what kind of work. The description, please," states Plateeney.

The Channel says, "Say you have a bad day as a human... A horrible day. Say you eat something that just happens to be modified or processed a certain way. Say there is something in an item that is a bi-product. We are inside the product, and you have no idea we are there because we are not labeled. It's like you have a vaccine, and there was mercury in it, and you didn't know it was there because it was hidden. That is us. You wouldn't be aware of us at all. You don't understand how we work together either. We are the ones that are entirely in stealth. You would never be aware of us at all."

"Say you start gaining weight, and you don't know why. You do everything correctly. You eat right, continue to start a fitness routine, and nothing seems to work. Your body will reach a particular range when you take on certain foods. That is when you can become vulnerable due to what you eat. If you don't eat food, you are supposed to eat. We can make you feel a certain way now if you feel aggravated because you can't lose weight when you come in. The aggravation that sets in is her."

"Basically, it's the whisperer. It's like a whisper that regularly states a thought, "I am aggravated," or "I am worthless," slowly to the person's mind. So slowly, we are masters of waiting. We wait slowly to attack. We are the first method of you becoming pulsed for an entity to move forward. You prep the host and open the body up for entity movement. The entity is not something we want to be around. So to be involved with entity placement kind of pisses us off."

Agent Eph asks: "Are you Entities?"

"We are just having fun," says the channel.

Agent Eph asks: "Yes, but are you considered entities?

The Channel Entity states: "We would be considered entities by others, yes, but we are regarded as one entity, even though we are two."

Plateeney asks: "You work together... Can you work separately?"

The Entity says: "No."

Plateeney says: "So it takes two of you to accomplish your jobs?"

The Channel Entity says: "Yes, One is a female aspect, and the other is male. We work with both angles through their emotions, and we do not have an issue if you are interested in the same sex... that's why we are so effective. We are brilliant when it comes to the opposite sexes, as well. If you are male, we know how to work you from that aspect of a woman. And if you are into women, we know how to work that situation from a man's perspective. This allows you to envision extra things in your brain."

"We know how to manipulate the thoughts of the mind. If you are a man and 'into' men, we can make you believe that there is a fantasy that you may be interested in men for. You may not have that interest at all.

We know how to move you forward to react by stepping into something new sexually. This can confuse you, make you vulnerable on another level, and help us implement more activity through other outside Entities. The same goes for the woman's life as well."

Agent Eph asks: "Would you move them to be more interested in men if another man or woman would think they are already interested? And you just kind of take over that mindset?"

The Channel Entity: "We can enhance this attraction to the same sex if needed. In the same way, you have an addiction. It takes twenty-one days to be addicted to something. If you eat the same food twenty-one days in a row, you are addicted to that food in some way or subconsciously. If that food is not something proper for your body to digest.

I am just giving you an example; it's not just food. It is prescriptions, too. If you take one for thirty days. If you do yoga for thirty days or work out as well. Anything that makes you say I have to do this. We work underneath a source here but still await someone to see it. We are usually there before the obsession entity comes in and gives you the idea to do it. We set the stage for more issues at a later date. We prepare the ground for longevity in the host."

Agent Eph asks: "Would you say that homosexuality would be an obsession?"

The Channel Entity replies, "I would say that homosexuality is not an Entity process. But if you think to touch another man or woman, then you have the idea, and we get excited and make you elaborate on this."

Agent Eph asks: "Then the sexual entity comes in?"

The Channel Entity states: "The entity can come in, but we have to lay the foundation."

Agent Eph: "So the sexual entity can come in, and then you work more. When the Sexual Entity comes in to do her work, we are nowhere near this. They like to work alone, as well. We collaborate with all of them, but obsession is usually the one that comes in first. The obsession only goes if one entity cannot work with another. Allow an entity to take you entirely over like seven times. The other entity will probably find another host. But if a host is not confident, we will ensure that an entity controls this process before leaving. Depending on the phases are the way the world works."

Plateeney says: "Like the phases of the moon?"

The Channel Entity says: "Yes. You are also more susceptible to being under our control during these times. Does this make sense?"

Agent Eph says: Yeah, for example, in a full moon, would you have more control?

The Channel Entity says: "If it's a full moon, we don't have control at that time. Here is where it gets more interesting. A parasite will lay its eggs on or near a full moon. Now, we will open the nutrition channels for that parasite to feed. Whenever that happens, something could be different at that time. You will blame it on something else, and we can put those messages in your mind to make you think differently. We can put words in your mind to confuse you completely. So if you would say something like, I am hungry. Then we would open it up to make you even more hungry. Then you may eat a second time. And if you don't want to, we may try to open up the thought for you to enjoy it again. On a full moon, the parasites are already there. If you were aware of this information, we would strengthen his thoughts. It's easy for them to implement these ideas because you usually sleep when this occurs. Let's say this: we can communicate with the parasite."

"We then tell it this is the time to do what you do, and when that happens, your body will get tired, or something is wrong with you. It's easier to give a thought; we already know it's something as simple as being tired."

"We already know and continue to add affirmations in your mind with thoughts like "You're worthless," You're nothing." It's no different than playing the same song repeatedly. So you keep up the same patterns."

"Then you memorize the words in the song. Imagine this in your subconscious. But you are not aware of any of this because you are sleeping. As this happens, you become restless and an insomniac. You may have a nightmare because my friend always tells you what you don't want to hear while sleeping. We would also have to change our entire protocol if you could change a couple of regular patterns. If you eat healthily, we can't do anything about that. The body understands weight the same way a nutritionist knows what the body needs. We are aware of how to survive in courses without the body. Think of us as the smartest Ph.D. in dietetics in the world. We can quickly read the enzymes and bloodstream like a frequency to move where we need to go throughout the body to survive."

Agent Eph says: "So you may be healthy on this end. You may come out at a different angle."

The Channel Entity: Yes, that's precisely what we do. You may drink alcohol once a year, and if you do, we will try and figure out what we must do to make it happen again. Maybe twice or three times a year, we constantly work against humans. For example, we might send attractive signals (frequencies) to call you on the phone and wait for someone to send you the message to go out and drink. We may stimulate you to do so. We signal your brain that you may crave a drink to go out and enjoy yourself. The keyword is desired because it would be a human red flag to know that it's not part of their natural output for things. It's like an external signal that you need something from the outside, "the craving," and you should know we are in the works at that time.

Another great example is craving sex. The only reason you may be craving sex is that we sent a signal to your brain that you may feel like you need some the night before while sleeping. And believe it or not, depending on what you put in your body makes you all these things. Agent Eph asks: Food plays a significant role in humans' free will.

The Channel Entity says that food is everything, and it helps us work remotely even better. Mainly what you eat. Plateeney says that food is fundamental to a human's mental and physical health, in the aspect of being taken over like a parasite.

The Channel Entity: The parasite does not care what it is eating. If you eat a lot of bad food, there is nothing to flush the parasite out, and it will utilize the best part of your overall natural nutrition. So, if you don't cleanse yourself regularly, these parasites will always make you believe you are healthy. You can eat the best meat in the world, which does not matter because the parasite is eating it. And once you stop, then the parasite will change its angle and find another part of you that it can survive on. Then, we come in as an entity and work together to figure out what to do. It's almost like she (the whisper) is left, and I am on the right (the channel). She will work whenever I am not working, but I can step in anytime. It's the way it works.

Agent Eph: I have a clearer picture of how the whisperer works, but I would like to get a bigger picture of how the channeler works.

The Channel Entity: OK, say you go to your yoga class, and your yoga teacher instructs you on something. Yoga instructors are engaging because people generally go out globally and always want to help something or someone. People go out there (the world) and try to find a purpose, which may not even be their goal. Sometimes, this may help the entity more than you may know. So, say someone wants to be an instructor to help people feel better. If you sit down and create an energy field around a group of individuals, especially strangers.

Then you start saying, "We want to bring in the positive energy." Bringing in any energies outside your body or yourself, especially with a group of people, creates a more vital force in the room. Then, it is possible to make yourself vulnerable automatically because you allow your subconscious, through the ritual, to believe that your subconscious is letting whatever is in the room come in. When you do this, you are channeling energy and inviting it. Does this make sense?

Agent Eph: I hear what you are saying, and I think I understand, but I know when people are praying or asking for help, they will ask for God, Jesus, or something guiding them. How are you sure who is talking to you? I don't know for a while. I went to God, then God and Jesus, and I find myself as I learn more that I am just looking.

The Channel Entity asks, "Have you ever created sacred space before or while doing this? Do you know what sacred space is? You would create an encirclement or a seal to think of two triangles overlapping. The center of these two triangles creates a pattern. If you are sitting in the middle of these two patterns, you are seated in the space. If you are not doing this (sacred space) in some way every time, you are making yourself vulnerable. Whenever I feel an Entity or a ghost of what humans consider an apparition or spirit."

"They could be good or bad, and you are in a room calling in energy to help you with a fitness and full-body workout. Then that may "not" exactly be an excellent idea. A full-body routine opens up the chakras; if you are conjuring something, you are not protecting yourself. Then you are just asking to be taken over that much faster. I, as an Entity, can communicate what is happening inside of you while you are making yourself vulnerable. I can learn its intentions and speak to you on behalf of this frequency.

Agent Eph: So many are reaching out to a God, Jesus, or whoever they pray to; what can they do?

The Channel Entity: They can learn to create a seal of protection because they are not adequately educated and remain vulnerable until they do. Agent Eph: Nobody does that.

The Channel Entity: You are susceptible to problems if you don't do it. Agent Eph: So what if I am in church? What do you think a priest does in church? Why do you think the priest will not allow you to approach the altar as he prepares the body of Christ as a ritual? Why do you say?

Agent Eph: So, as I am in prayer in church?

Channel Entity: You see, right now, you are vulnerable.

Agent Eph: I need some clarification. It's because you are scared that you are not doing it right.

Agent Eph: I want to challenge it because I don't understand. This is the most significant problem humans have; they think they know everything, making them even more vulnerable. But the problem is you have been lied to for many years,

Channel Entity: You are supposed to create sacred space before doing anything. Agent Eph: No one knows this. Agent Eph: So you are telling me that when we pray in a group or have bible study, we are laying our hands on someone and praying for that person and asking for help.

Channel Entity: No one is supposed to. We love it. This is how we can take over more aspects of many people. God makes you vulnerable.

Agent Eph: I am just not buying this.

Channel Entity: Well, I am telling you that if you do not create sacred space, and you ask for anything outside of yourself to help you without your sacred space and protection, then yes, you are leaving yourself vulnerable.

Agent Eph: So, how do you perform sacred space? You have to do the same thing a priest does at the altar. I wasn't listening; I was too mesmerized while thinking I had been misinformed all these years. Maybe a little in shock.

Agent Eph: Which is what? Channel Entity: Whenever a priest walks around spraying before church...and into the church, you can smell a scent...why do you think they do this? Why do you believe there are candles in the church? Why do you think they are lit during the ritual before you receive them. The fragrances you usually smell are frankincense and myrrh.

Agent Eph: So you must go through this whole routine, and what if you need to pray immediately. If you feel this way, you may want to do something other than it. Suppose you are actually in a dangerous place. In that case, you should escape that location before opening up in a hostile environment. It's even more harmful. You don't sit there and start praying in a hostile environment.

Agent Eph: I feel like I communicate with God all the time, and I just feel like it's a lesson to be learned if you keep making yourself vulnerable. Here is an example: Hollywood has made everyone dumb because you may have a movie like an exorcist. They don't show you anything. You have a woman who got possessed, and a priest comes in and tries to save her. That's it. So basically, all they did was show you that you make yourself vulnerable until the ability to have this thing wait until you are powerless to take you over. That's precisely what it does. Does this make sense?

Agent Eph: I am resisting it. Channel Entity: You can do that all day. Let me explain: All they did was show you how to make yourself vulnerable. When you get close to an entity, you can wait. When you start studying and learning more about this, it does and will make more sense. Let me explain this: The priest has anointed oil.

Agent Eph: Does the priest know about this? Yes, Agent Eph: Why wouldn't he allow others to know this? Because the funny thing about you humans is that you feel. You want. You can just do it. In the same way, a yoga teacher teaches three classes, and then she believes she can teach the whole class effectively.

Agent Eph: But prayer is such an essential thing for many. It's also very secretive. They do not want everybody to know. It's all about control with them, too.

Agent Eph: I always watch videos, and people ask guides and angels. I have heard you say it, and I never create a sacred space. Then you probably never will, which makes you continuously vulnerable. If you go to a church and go into church practice regularly. Depending on the church and how it was built, you will automatically be walking into a place of worship with sacred space, but not all have this. This is what is so special about many churches of the past.

Today, they are certainly not all created equal. But you have to ask yourself: Do you feel safe in church? The auras and energy of the people feeling good and positive are still there. It's peaceful, I hear many humans say. But if the only place that sacred space is created is around the altar, I would certainly be questioning the pastor or priest in the church that day. But why would you believe me? I am just an entity. If they sat there and taught you all these things, you may feel like you don't need to attend church. That's why you feel safe. When you go to church. I am telling you, I cannot exist unless you know this.

Agent Eph: OK, You asked me a question. I answered it; it's not the answer you wanted.

Agent Eph: I'm trying to figure it out. There is nothing to figure out.

Agent Eph: How do we seal ourselves off? But you are supposed to tell us.

Channel Entity: But "You" have to understand I am not a bringer of the "positive" light, and it's not my job to tell you that. And a priest will not say either. He will just agree. But realistically, he has to create sacred space before doing anything of ritual in the church and sometimes outside it. I say this because he may have the cloak of sacred space he created for himself.

Agent Eph: You are telling me that no one should pray? Unless they have sacred space. You better have a sacred space around you before you talk to anything. Agent Eph: What if it's what you say that God is within? Your soul does not exist inside your body, so think about that momentarily. Then, you will have to figure out what's within it.

Agent Eph: OK, now tell me about holy water. It changes what the water does whenever you bless holy water or anything with intent, whether right or wrong. The same way you change "you" when you look in a mirror and give it a thought. When you look at "you with a thought," you change your water. Here is an example: Your organs are within your body. Because your body is made up of a large sum of water, when you intend to bless yourself, you also bless the water in your body. Does that make sense?

OK... you can think of your skin as a sacred space. There is nothing that can affect the organs in the body. Is that correct? If you are thinking of it this way, does it make sense? When you drink something, what do you just do? Agent Eph: You are filling your body with a liquid. Channel Entity: That's doing what? Agent Eph: It nourishes your body? Channel Entity: What if it's not nourishing or clean?

Agent Eph: Then it is not suitable for you? If it can educate you, you have to feel good about it. How will you honestly argue with me about what was just said? Especially if you did not feel optimistic about what entered your body?

Agent Eph: Do you have to create a ritual of creating sacred space? You have to cleanse everything. You don't have to make a ceremony, it's up to you however you choose.

Agent Eph: Can you ask it to cleanse stuff? Channel Entity: This makes sense to you.

Agent Eph: A little...yes. Channel Entity: Now you understand the purpose of why they ever started saying grace. Agent Eph: Do you have to create a sacred space to ask for prayer? Yes, but not for food?

Channel Entity: Everything is a natural resource from God. Think of it this way.

Agent Eph: Do you have to create a sacred place before you are intimate with anything you want to ask for in a prayer form? Or should you make some sacred space within yourself before regarding your entire body?

Channel Entity: It can be done mentally, and it can be done visually. The more that you do, the more it helps you.

Agent Eph: But you can do it visually, and it can be effective?

Channel Entity: Yes. And it can be just as powerful.

Agent Eph: Yes. OK, If it were not, then holy water would not exist. There would be no such thing.

Agent Eph: Now I feel a little better about this. I was not happy about this situation. I wanted to punch you. I am just telling you the truth.

Channel Entity: This is the theory about how you are programmed and what you see. This is also an understanding of how stubborn you humans can be. The data you have is dated. If it were not BS, we would not be having this conversation. I would not be on this planet.

Agent Eph: No one ever taught us how to create sacred space.

Channel Entity: No one ever taught you how to cleanse your home with holy water. But you have it in your home. So what are you going to do with it?

Agent Eph: I do have some.

Channel Entity: Do you really think that your holy water in the dresser of your home tucked away will get rid of evil spirits? Not at all.

Agent Eph: You have to spray it around. Channel Entity: What are you doing when you pour it around? Agent Eph: Creating sacred space?

Channel Entity: Ahh, Thank you, Eph.

Agent Eph: Is there a prayer, or do you just sprinkle it around?

Channel Entity: The fact that it is holy water, that's it. However, it was blessed to create sacred space if used correctly. Think shapes and symbols.

Agent Eph: OK, how does water get holy?

Channel Entity: You must create a ritual of blessings within yourself to add it to the water like you would pray to yourself from within. Similarly, you can create a sacred space around your entire home. Your home can be blessed because you and your family are inside that home. The reason it's called a home? It is that of God... an active symbol. God is supposed to be a symbol of positivity. "Where you are safe." Today, in many homes in America, owners need to learn about sacred space. So, do many of them have safe containment around them? This can create a portal on the front and the rear door that allows interdimensional frequencies to enter the home. What exactly do entities exist on?

Agent Eph: Yes, those frequencies.

Channel Entity: Even if we don't enter this way, you are just opening up more crazy energy if one person walks into your home tainted the same way your body is and can be corrupted. It's the same process.

Agent Eph: The holy water in my home comes from a Catholic church. Is this sacred water?

Channel Entity: It depends on the priest because not all priests are precisely holy. You should understand they can have entities in them also. Being judgemental is an excellent way to open yourself up to entities.

Agent Eph asks, Is that a separate entity or thing?

Channel Entity: It's very similar. It's more what "she" (the whisperer) does.

Agent Eph: That probably came from a judgemental place, and I want this to be more exact. How can you question what can't be because who is the thing?

Agent Eph: Right.

Channel Entity: You know, as entities and as observers, we know what you do wrong. We see what you do regularly. You are programmed to love, fight, create anger, judge, and think. But you are not scheduled to take the existence of your internal self.

Agent Eph: Yes, we are not taught here to build (the brain) that muscle for sure.

Channel Entity: How can you truly know what "don't" is? Agent Eph: People struggle with that one. You know what it is when you get deep internally.

Channel Entity: God is not a God if I exist; it tells me if I live in this composition. Conversing with me will make you question God five times if you can go to sleep and question everything you do. Then it would make you ask God again with "who" is one of the things you do.

Agent Eph: You guys make us question God?

Channel Entity: Yes... because it makes you even more vulnerable. But we hope it actually makes you smarter, too. The only place you can get anywhere near sacred space is a church. So the more we drive you away from it, the more you will never question a priest about sacred space. You have to go to seminary school or through the "don't" channels to understand what that means. Because to understand the entity... how it was built, and what it has been constructed on. You are not aware of any of this stuff.

Agent Eph: Is a Catholic church the only sacred space? What about satanic churches? Any church?

Channel Entity: If they create sacred space, they are safe. Agent Eph: I know if that is the case.

Channel Entity: Well, they may or could do it another way, but if they are not creating sacred space or did not build the church on top of holy space symbols or elements, it is highly questionable. There is a ritual involved also. The only thing about them having a different church is that they have practices also. The satanic church does the same thing.

Agent Eph: So creating a sacred place is a good thing. Creating a sacred space or place keeps you from being vulnerable.

Agent Eph: Got it.

Channel Entity: Here is where it gets interesting. Everything. If you were to walk through a satanic church, everything about it is a ritual. The term ritual Catholics fear that word but do it the second they walk into their church.

Agent Eph: They are not even aware of it. Precisely, and they judge everyone else. The funniest thing the world made humans believe was that the devil existed. The devil does not even exist.

Agent Eph, does evil exist?

Channel Entity: Evil to me does not exist.

Agent Eph: What is the purpose of having an entity if evil does not exist? So we can survive?

Channel Entity: That's the way we see it. We look at it as helping you because you are asking this question.

Agent Eph: What if you didn't exist. Would we be better off?

Channel Entity: We think you wouldn't be at all. Experiencing things how we like to think could be better. But just because we exist, we also know we have to survive.

Agent Eph: So you say the devil does not exist. Evil does not exist. Do evil spirits exist?

Channel Entity: Here is the most confusing thing when sitting down and praying. You may need to be aware of fifteen others who prayed in the same place or location and how they were mentally ill. And also what they were praying for or to whom.

Agent Eph: OK. Channel Entity: If you see your mom, who died a year ago, come to you in a room visually, and she reaches her hands out to you in a dream or in reality. You see... this makes you vulnerable. A. or B. is going to happen. A. You'll reach out and accept her as your mother to hold your hand, or you will open yourself up and be afraid. Either way, you hold yourself by opening your hand, afraid or not. You are still vulnerable because you have no idea if your mother is.

Agent Eph: What would be a way you wouldn't be vulnerable in that situation?

Channel Entity: First, you would create a sacred space around you. Then you would say to whatever was in front of you. "If you are not in the best interest of my sacred space, please leave.

Agent Eph: Thank you.

Channel Entity: That's the best way to explain it. You control yourself. You have free will. Your vulnerability is how we exist. The fact that so many of you on this planet are so vulnerable has allowed us to be here to evolve for hundreds of years. You are so much in control that it isn't even funny. Still, it gets interesting if you are not appropriately educated on what matters and allow you to move forward after you pass on. Your soul passes to the next dimension; how the hell are you going to get there?

How do you think things are walking around this planet now? Because none of them can close how to get there, just don't think heaven does not allow you to automatically get there. What if you leave and decide you know where you are going. How do you control that your soul may not be on auto-pilot? You don't control your body; how will you maintain your soul?

Agent Eph: Do you know they don't speak of souls that move on?

Channel Entity: I don't know that information.

Agent Eph: Do you believe that a low number of souls move on?

The Channel Entity: I believe that the majority of souls are lost. Just as lost as they are in the state you are in while you live.

Agent Eph: Do they eventually gain knowledge floating around? The Channel Entity: They eventually gain information while traveling to channel dimensions. They ultimately gain more experience from following others. Now, if you follow another that just so happens to need to know where they are going, where are you going? It's no different than the blind leading the blind. The whole reason you are sitting where you are sitting right now, asking me questions now, is that we are trying to change that. As much as we survive off of you, we feel pretty bad for you because you are so vulnerable. Think of it as a challenge.

Agent Eph: So, you are challenging us to move on quicker. Channel Entity: Yes.

Agent Eph: As we leave our body?

Channel Entity: Absolutely!

Agent Eph: OK.

Agent Eph explains: This is more of a pleasant conversation even though it didn't start that way with the other entities. Only because the information you gave me didn't make sense to me, but now I understand a little more.

Channel Entity: Once your ego stops, your comprehension ability is better.

Agent Eph: Right... I had to ask a few more questions to visualize the whole purpose of understanding this information for one reason. You are no different than us. We exist through you because your soul is also an entity.

Agent Eph: Our soul is an entity?

Channel Entity: Your soul takes on a vessel. What do we do?

Agent Eph: Yeah, but the pure soul without the host in the body is entity-free.

Channel Entity: The body is not entity-free. The soul without the body is entity-free.

Agent Eph: Yes. You see "Eph" as a channeler; what can we channel without creating a sacred space?

Agent Eph: That could be a problem in our life.

Channel Entity: You create enough chaos in your life. We don't need to do that.

Agent Eph: What is the purpose of being a channeler entity?

Channel Entity: The purpose of being a channeler entity is to communicate with the one we open the door to. We are the landlord, "Eph," so you hope we don't create a sacred space. Well, we know you are not going to.

Agent Eph: OK, so that's making us an easier target.

Channel Entity: Very easy, Yes. Agent Eph: So basically, knock on the door, and here we are.

Agent Eph: So do we... "By not creating the sacred space," do we draw in negative spirits and negativity?

Channel Entity: You definitely bring in some negative frequencies.

Agent Eph: What is that, though?

Channel Entity: It could be a negative soul, someone interested in your light body, or a possible entity. It's no different than a woman who loves a diamond. You may have a spirit that views you the same way. You may be shining like a diamond. And she was used to seeing five hundred people in a day who had to look at her ring. She may think you are excited and may just wanna spend the day with you. You will and won't even know if she gets attached, but you will learn something different.

Agent Eph: Are spirits entities?

Channel Entity: Spirits can be entities, yes.

Agent Eph: They can have entities but are not the primary entity to do the work.

Agent Eph: So, a harmful spirit would be something evil?

Channel Entity: If your soul controlled your body and was happy, it's what you would consider being yourself. So, it could be a soul that has not passed on and is just content or unhappy about life. Not evil, because evil does not exist, actually. Yes, it's evil to you. It's not evil to them.

Agent Eph: Evil is an objective but not really anything that exists.

Channel Entity: The church created the terms good and evil for control. And I will tell you this. The control aspect of everything was also set up by the church. To make you never question sacred space, the real question to me would be: Is the church involved?

Agent Eph: I would like to see if Plateeney has any more questions for the two of you.

Plateeney: I have a question for her. (whisper entity) Why has she not said anything yet?

Channel Entity: She does not feel she needs to speak.

Plateeney: She has never moved from looking at Agent Eph the whole time. How does that make you feel, Eph?

Agent Eph: Now that you tell me, it seems a little creepy, but I was involved in the questioning earlier. But now that I think about it, I am curious why.

Channel Entity: You remember how you were asking about the soul and spirits moving on? You can think of her like that. You can think of her like that in that way. Someone who is waiting for you to be vulnerable. Anyone who will wait for you to be vulnerable is not really your friend.

Agent Eph: Those are powerful words. It's simple but compelling because so many humans hit you when you are vulnerable.

Channel Entity: That's what she is; she will make you react when you are vulnerable.

Agent Eph: You are susceptible even when you have an ego in that state.

Channel Entity: There are control and elements of power. Until the day you die. It gets older if you just release that your body is not even there. Then you would be a lot better. The whole point is that we are here together. God exists. The world has become fixated that God is "there." God has never left. He's always there. The fact that "I am" communicating to you to help humanity understand how we control you would be an excellent indication of God's existence. The saddest part about it is the church that's so controlling... I couldn't tell you that. No one in power will admit their faults unless forced to by some force. Even God is within a whisper connection. I believe it's true because I exist. Agent Eph: But you don't want us to believe in God.

Channel Entity: I don't care what you believe. Look at the numbers. You're an agent trained to ask me questions. You are one of the most influential people because it's the first time anyone has ever been able to ask us questions. It's the first time anyone has ever seen what we are in containment. We exist in an entirely different dimension that you cannot even comprehend. So many humans are scared of the word "dimension." You cannot even handle this. How are you going to deal with death?

Agent Eph: Oh yeah, death scares me a little.

Channel Entity: Because they think that's its death. That's not it at all. You have more control over death than you do when you are alive. You have more power as a soul or a person of thought than when you are in your body.

Agent Eph: Death to me; the more I learn about it, I am not scared and want to live a long life, maybe until nearly a hundred years. It is a better life. There is so much I want to do while I'm here.

Channel Entity: Does that mean every time? You will understand what God is whenever you can be a soul. There is no judgment, no questioning. There is nothing.

Agent Eph: Is there an expansion of knowledge getting closer to your soul?

Channel Entity: It's not a part of anything about your body. Agent Eph: Just the spirit.

Channel Entity: See, here are all of these questions... When you are a soul, you don't question anything. Agent Eph: Cause you just know?

Channel Entity: The fact that you are moving is God. You just know. You become an utterly clairsentient ball of dust. There is no question. Just the fact there is no question or feeling is God. All humans would consider heaven, but no one has that ability in a body. A body will always have parasites and entities. Whenever you can leave the aspect of who you are inside and experience a higher dimension, that's what you talk about when you are a soul...you just don't speak.

Agent Eph: The closer we get there... It may be more challenging for the whisperer to do their job.

Channel Entity: Because we are not vulnerable. When you are not powerless, you live in a state of love within yourself because you constantly change the aspect of your life. People who live in competition and repetition only make themselves more vulnerable because they are stressed out. That is the constant stream of people they will be attracted to. This system is designed against you from the start.

Agent Eph: People that live in a state of no growth.

Channel Entity: Yeah. Agent Eph: You need new experiences. If you are not growing, you are failing.

Channel Entity: Why do you think you are here in the first place? It's not to die. It's to live. If we attach to humans, their lives have to have some meaning. It's the truth because half of them have an attachment in the first place because they hate their lives. We see it as if we are doing you a favor. We are spicing it up, but simultaneously, we are surviving. We are living through you. You think it's you, but it's not.

Agent Eph: Wow.

Channel Entity: When we get tired of you. You may just get an STD or an arrest warrant. You never know, but that's our way of saying somebody else is moving in.

Agent Eph: Can we see if she will talk or say anything?

Channel Entity: You can try.

Plateeney: Does she have a name?

Channel Entity: No

Agent Eph: I want you to say whatever is on your mind. Something that could be helpful to us right now.

Channel Entity: She thinks that you are familiar with her. Yes

Agent Eph: Why... so I mainly know. Is that why she is staring at me?

Channel Entity: Yes, it is.

Agent Eph: Is she threatened by me? I'm curious.

Channel Entity: She has no thought at all. She just feels like you are very familiar to her. She has been a part of you before.

Agent Eph: Like she has been my whisperer entity?

Channel Entity: Yes, basically. Agent Eph: So there are several of you. Are you just representing the channeler and the whisperer or more?

Agent Eph: Can you ask her what part of the negative crap was a part of her in my lifetime?

Channel Entity: The first time you shot someone. Agent Eph is silent, waits about 30 seconds, and says... OK.

Agent Eph: Well, that was when I was twelve, and I shot a tree, and it ricocheted and hit my sister in the forehead from a nearby tree. I aimed at a tree, and the bullet bounced and hit my sister directly in the forehead. That was it for me with guns for a while.

Channel Entity: How did you feel about guns after that, Agent Eph? I hated them.

Channel Entity: What do you think of them now?

Agent Eph: I still hate them. Not only that. I remember shooting a shotgun with my father a year later, which sealed the deal with the loud noise. It freaked me out. These two incidents changed my life. I don't want one, still to this day.

Channel Entity: OK. How do you feel about people that don't have a problem with guns?

Agent Eph: Family members were fascinated with them. I'm OK with it and feel a little protected now.

Channel Entity: Do you think you are protected because you have a gun?

Agent Eph: I haven't ever thought I was protected because of having or not having a gun. I don't judge people with them; it's just not something I care for much. I came from a family with a hunting background, and there were always many of them around. I just never needed one. The danger is something I always disliked.

Channel Entity: OK...Everything you told me about made you vulnerable since you were eleven. Do you understand how you have been vulnerable?

Agent Eph: Did you know all this before I told you yes? Is that how you know me?

Channel Entity: No... but that is how we work together. We make you believe something you need protects you, but you have no reason to like it. The fact that you made "the gun" do something is what you don't want inside of you. The gun did not do anything. You pulled the trigger. It's a trauma... just like today.

Agent Eph: Just like today?

Channel Entity: Now you realize you hated something because there was nothing. So you take the years, add them up, and figure out how long you have been vulnerable.

Agent Eph: Well, a gun is a danger to me.

Channel Entity: It's a danger, but it's not, especially if it has no bullets. It's just a sense of what you believe.

Agent Eph: I guess so.

Channel Entity: Yeah... The trauma affected you when you were eleven and still affects you now.

Agent Eph: Yeah, because I know it bothers me. You have been vulnerable that long.

Agent Eph: Is that when the whisperer came into my life?

Channel Entity: The whisperer entity told you to pull the trigger before you even drew it.

Agent Eph: I was not aiming at her directly.

Channel Entity: It does not matter. If we didn't affect you, we would affect those around you. Just to get to you. It is not why you were vulnerable. It's no different than someone at war closing in on an enemy. Every single thing in your body does the same thing. It's how cancer grows. It's how the flu nourishes itself to take over your body. It figures out a way to do it. So, putting things aside and not giving them an honest thought on exactly how you are supposed to move forward instead of just saying you dealt with them means you are still vulnerable.

There is no perfect parent, which means there is no perfect human. Many parents have yet to learn what to teach their children, whether right or wrong. It's the simplest thing, and usually, it comes from childhood.

Agent Eph: Does she remember how she knows me yet?

Channel Entity: I think she figured it out. Agent Eph: Can she tell me what it is?

Channel Entity: She does not want to talk.

Agent Eph: Was it the gun?

Channel Entity: It was not the gun. It was the thought. Her job is to open you up.

Agent Eph: So she was the whisperer that told me to shoot the weapon. Did she ever come back?

Channel Entity: She didn't need to. She did her job. That's all she needed to do. How old are you now?

Agent Eph: A few weeks shy of age forty-seven. Channel Entity: How long was that? Agent Eph: Thirty-five years.

Channel Entity: How do you feel knowing you have been vulnerable that long?

Agent Eph: It makes sense. I see images of women attending rifle practice, sometimes making me nauseated to even think about it. I know that it's part of my life. I shouldn't feel that way, but I would need therapy.

Channel Entity: In over 30 years, why did you not seek help? The fact that you didn't go does not mean that you didn't need therapy. Agent Eph: I have been for other things, but not for this.

Channel Entity: Has it ever come up in therapy?

Agent Eph: No... just simple questions. Channel Entity: Even then, a therapist could not evaluate the issue.

Agent Eph: But it was a different matter altogether.

Channel Entity: Do you think this issue affected other issues you may have had?

Agent Eph: Yes, it could have. I remember before then. It does make sense I was carefree. I would walk to the edge of a mountain and never get scared. I would flip off diving boards with no fear, and then twelve and thirteen, I started being fearful twelve and thirteen.

Channel Entity: How do you know your life will be different due to the knowledge you now know.

Agent Eph: Having this knowledge and pinpointing where the fear comes from... I can say, OK... this is it.

Channel Entity: How would you have felt if you had killed your sister with the gun?

Agent Eph: I would have been emotionally crippled for the rest of my life.

Channel Entity: Who is to say you have not been?

Agent Eph: Yes, I understand. Just going that close to her face freaked me out.

Channel Entity: When you shoot a gun, a gun is outside of yourself. It's still outside of yourself. What I'm telling you is this... "Anything" outside of yourself should not allow you to be taken over, and if it does, it's not of God.

Agent Eph: Powerful.

Channel Entity: Only when the bullet enters the interior of who you are... that's when you experience God.

Agent Eph: Explain.

Channel Entity: Two things are going to happen. One, the bullet enters the interior of the body. You will either move forward and learn if your life is spared, or you will die both ways you experience God, and so will the person who shoots.

Agent Eph: True.

Channel Entity: The second you break the sacred space, you encounter God, good or bad.

Agent Eph: Was she there when the second accident happened? When I almost hurt my sister a second time that year. Do you know what it is? Not the gun.

Channel Entity: Something physical, that's all I got? I mean, did you hit her with something?

Agent Eph: No, we were fishing, and my parents and I cast my pole and hooked her in the face close to the same area. It was not long after. At least a year, within a year. We joke about this now, but it was pretty bad.

Channel Entity: Nothing would physically dictate that you physically did that to hurt someone. That was your thought manifesting. Agent Eph: Got you.

Channel Entity: This was a great therapy session for sure. It's not that we want to kill you. You live half of your life unknown where you want to go. We honestly feel bad. We do. The rest of the entities are similar to me; I can't speak for them. We experience life with you. We are as close to your human existence as you are. You just don't know it.

Agent Eph: Is there any time the whisperer entity will back off because we can't handle it?

Channel Entity: The Whisperer will not speak until "it or she" feels ready.

Agent Eph: You can speak for the whisperer then...is there a time when they will back off because the person is depressed?

Channel Entity: If a person is in depression, it's because the whisperer entity got to them. They will only slack off once an entity makes its home in a person. They will not slack off at all. Whenever we go, we move out, and they move in.

Agent Eph: When a whisperer entity does its programming for a person. It usually means reacting negatively.

Channel Entity: Or to allow an addiction or entity to come in. Yes. It's programmed because it's an addiction at that point. I don't know all because I sometimes have the same body as the entity. But if you constantly hear "you are a failure" in your sleep, you will think, "You are a failure." After thirty days, you will start to say, "I can't do this." Then we are just getting you ready for an entity. We are the key masters of the entity. You can call us this. We are the masters of getting them placed.

Agent Eph: Like a job placement service for entities.

Channel Entity: That's what we do. We exist. We don't feed on you the same way they do. We live and are existent to allow them to exist. The only difference between you and me is I am being forced to answer questions against my will. But we understand what you go through because we constantly watch what you deal with in the human body.

Agent Eph: That's true. Is she still staring at me? Is there anything that's on her mind right now?

Channel Entity: Yes, she is staring. She is fixated on seeing anything. She does not get to see the same people again. She is trying to process that she jumps from one and moves on. Just because she is there and knows your energy, she knows you. It's like a memory for her. She does not know how to process that. It's different from what she was designed and programmed to do. Like you and me, you can think of her as someone you knew that's not at all there. Mainly because she is not at all there. Her program is basically to wait in a closet until you get home.

Agent Eph: Does she ever communicate verbally.

Channel Entity: She whispers... that's what she does. Say if you are a depressed or sexual person, you get horny. (being a sexual person) It doesn't matter what you are doing if you are experiencing sexuality in any way. Take puberty in general. The whisper entity is probably around that time. And that's why it happened when you were eleven years old. That's right around the time we show up. The ego pops right out.

Agent Eph: I'm fascinated by her, maybe because she's not talking.

Channel Entity: See, here's the thing you need to understand. She's not talking because she doesn't need to speak. You can close your mind, look within yourself, and talk to her. You don't have to talk to me. That's how she's programmed. She is scheduled to speak to "your" mind. I mean, you don't want to talk to her anyway?

Agent Eph: I do, though.

Channel Entity: But why? You're just allowing yourself to be more vulnerable.

Agent Eph: You are right. I don't, especially if she will try a trick or two.

Channel Entity: That is what she is programmed to do. She is not the same kind of entity as the others. She is not restricted like the others. I am just here.

Agent Eph: Why are you handcuffed?

Channel Entity: They don't want us to run around the building exactly.

Agent Eph: Why are there padded walls?

Channel Entity: The whisperer can control a person's thoughts if needed.

Agent EPH: You need padded walls for that?

Channel Entity: No, it's just where they put us in, thinking these walls have some frequency that disallows us to communicate with the other side. But I am unaware at this time. It's because of the level of control she has. Frequency is potent. It can even kill a human, which many people are unaware of.

Agent Eph: That's interesting.

Channel Entity: They can actually kill us too. We will only go near if a room has a high frequency. We are in that dimension, we can see. It's no different than what you would call a laser or something similar in its frequency. It's emitting something. The need for a microwave to heat something up and explode something while it's in that environment also... you don't think that's good for you, do you?

Agent Eph: Hmm, probably not. I need more questions.

Do you have anything? No, I am good.

Agent Eph: Thank you for being so open and thorough.

Channel Entity: Educate yourself before educating others.

Agent Eph: That makes sense.

Channel Entity: The reason we are doing what we are doing here. The reason this is happening at this time is. It's one part of your training and the second part for you to educate yourself on the "why." We can control all aspects of your lives; we are here. There is no other reason why we are here. If you are not educated, we don't exist.

Agent Eph: If we are not educated, we don't exist...

Channel Entity: Yes!

Agent Eph: That makes no sense.

Channel Entity: It makes a lot of sense.

Agent Eph: The more educated we are, the less likely you would be able to exist.

Channel Entity: The less educated we are, the more we exist. More entities exist, and there should be a balance. Education of ourselves would help create a balance.

Agent Eph: So, could you reverse that? Did you mean the opposite?

Channel Entity: No. I am saying that if you become extinct, you don't exist. We both become extinct. Does this make sense?

Agent Eph: We need each other on this planet?

Channel Entity: Yes,

Agent Eph: What would happen if we don't have you guys?

Channel Entity: You would eventually become extinct anyway.

Agent Eph: Is this part of the human journey or the learning process?

Channel Entity: No, it's usually called the law of polarity. It's not part of the learning life journey.

Agent Eph: Do we need these obstacles to exist?

Channel Entity: If you do not exist, you will become extinct.

Agent Eph: So, we need these barriers?

Channel Entity: You are not learning anything at this point. If you have yet to learn where you came from, how will you learn anything more significant? You still need to learn the history of anything. Half of the things that you do today are completely being wrongly guided. Many are false rituals. Half of the habits you know allow something else to gain more power over the human race. This is also controlled by us.

Agent Eph: If we don't have chaos and things going on, we don't know, correct?

Channel Entity: Yes, that is right.

Agent Eph: We need that contrast to exist, and we can't reduce that negative, but to get there, we require that contrast.

Channel Entity: Silver is valuable because it makes you believe gold is more beneficial. The same goes for just about anything.

Agent Eph: I'm sure. Channel Entity: What does a diamond do?

Agent Eph: I don't know. Nothing?

Channel Entity: It's all just things, illusions. Please educate yourselves. Because you are becoming extinct.

Agent Eph: Just because we get better and educate ourselves, will it make us extinct?

Channel Entity: Eventually. If you get better, we cannot overpower you?

Agent Eph: I don't understand.

Channel Entity: I am trying to tell you that an entity will consume every part of who you are until you have nothing left.

Agent Eph: So we must educate ourselves to improve and have fewer entities.

Channel Entity: To better educate yourself is to understand why you exist. You don't even know what death is. An example is the purpose of saying Jesus is coming back. I hear humans say this all the time. If Jesus actually walked on the planet, what would you do?

Agent Eph: I would freak out, and most people would.

Channel Entity: Exactly! Because people today have no idea how to perceive it. Agent Eph: Many believers would freak out even though they wouldn't admit it.

Channel Entity: They would run because they don't know how to understand this would happen. Many people wouldn't admit that they wouldn't even know what to do, the same way the natives didn't know Columbus's ship because they had never seen one in the ocean. So, the first person who says he is Jesus and just so happens to make a miracle occur? What are they going to do? Believe it? They don't know what to believe today. They think the paper is valuable. The only thing the paper is relevant for is that you are reading it. I'll give you fifteen thousand papers, which will become more valuable because there is more than one. This does not make sense.

Agent Eph: Before we wrap up, can you give us a few examples of creating sacred space? Visually, but how?

Channel Entity: The people we could not contain would either go to a place they have created or use frequencies. They also primarily used patterns of triangles. Specific geometric designs can only handle some of those things.

Agent Eph: Can you visualize angels and white light around you?

Channel Entity: A human's intent is powerful. Whatever you intend to happen, if you intently put something around you, it usually does. It does not need to be an angel. It could be a force field. Whatever you believe, a force field makes it possible for you to contain yourself.

Agent Eph: So sacred is whatever you feel is safe, but it also has to have some meaning of what you believe. Ask yourself: Is the love you need to simultaneously be a state of this? Agent Eph: Surrounding myself with white angels?

Channel Entity: What is an angel? Is that what you believe an angel is or know one is? Today, most people would run if they saw an angel because it would be something they would not be used to. People are afraid of many things today in general. If we see someone full of light, we try to focus on them to have more fear at that point. You will probably have sexual problems because the sexual entity is the one that loves fear.

Agent Eph: What if I have angels around me? Channel Entity: It depends on asking the angels to come in the form. The way that I understand, I wouldn't ask anything from outside. I would surround myself, visualize the interior of my heart chakra, and surround myself with what I feel at peace.

Agent Eph: It's much easier to pray and not think about all that.

Channel Entity: I understand that, but once again, it's part of the procedure, and I will tell you something: the whole reason you hold a rosary is a ritual. The holding of anything is a ritual. Holding the rosary should speak volumes about the subconscious thought of doing. Just having the rosary itself is a sacred thing. It's holy because of the meanings behind it. For some, it's just a thing with some rocks on it. Many don't even know what it is. If you found a rosary in a case, what would you think that is? But yet, if you see a fire that's an element, then you know it has more meaning than rock.

You put meaning in things. So you should question the importance of everything around you because you will feel it. We are not all from the same place. And it's OK for us to be different. It's OK for us to look further. It's OK for us to feel different. But not everyone will feel the same way, and that's a significant part of where we are. And it's also a considerable part of why it's so important. But if we don't understand the balance, we will become extinct. It's not just you. It's even beyond that, but we know that part of this situation is that you are becoming extinct. Agent Eph: Getting this knowledge in myself and my partner makes you more conscious of your surroundings. Agent Eph: As we become more aware of this, can we teach others? We can lead others by example.

Agent Eph: OK.

Channel Entity: Today's examples do not teach anyone because you keep regurgitating the same outcome. Here is an example: If you are infested with five entities, and every human is infested with three, if you are a physicist, what do you think you will build infested with entities.

I mean, entities don't reflect on love. They don't know what that is now you understand more. You can't create anything as an entity if we are all entities here. We wouldn't need you. We can't exist in a lower population. We will look for the worst person in the town until we can corrupt more people. This is why we are in more problematic areas until we take them over and until "you" go to jail. We are not going to be a part of that. We will find somebody else on their way out of jail because we know they are accessible to corrupt. After all, they just got out of jail.

Agent Eph: I imagine you have already done the work.

Channel Entity: Some people get rid of us. They create sacred space, and they move forward. There is no reason to continue that journey until that changes. But at the rate you are going, you are headed for extinction.

Agent Eph: Right. I understand. Is there anything else? Plateeney: Are there any other questions? Do you have any more to say to us?

Channel Entity: Educate yourself.

Plateeney: OK. Thank You.

Entity 7

THE HUMAN ENTITY

Plateeney and Agent Eph are exhausted from the channel and whisper entities. After researching various information, we regroup and walk back in a similar person, except they are under complete entity control. We are cautious because it could be possible that this individual we are about to speak to is infested with 5 or more entities we interrogated. The human entity is a human with all the entities we have discussed to show us the worst-case scenario we may deal with in a real-life situation.

Agent Eph asks: A human monster of sorts?

Plateeney: I guess, yes.

Agent Eph: This will be just as scary as an entity because they are material.

Plateeney: We will be more protected, but you have to remember that this person will be contained. But if something happens, we are armed with guards in the room and trained to handle the situation if force is needed. I am not going to hesitate to shoot it. It's a person, so we can cross-reference them. We will be speaking to the person, then the entity. They may come and go, which may need clarification, but we will be alert and handle the situation as needed. We will actually have the ability to say we would like to speak to the entity in you. We are briefed that it will be the first time a human will give up his free will to allow the entities attached to him to discuss situations with us. This may also be a learning experience for all in the room because of its rare case. So, we know that the human entity will discuss highly realistic situations in life or beyond. He will talk about the things he has dealt with that have made him not want to be a part of his soul. It sounds crazy, but it will be weird and a learning experience in one. It's basically like interviewing a person who is possessed. It's like what a person would consider an exorcism while being interviewed. Agent Eph: This is the last day of our training before we go out and deal with this sort of thing in the real world, so let's see how crazy this can get.

Plateeney: It's supposed to be a life-changing experience. You ready, Yes.

Plateeney and Eph approach a door that resembles an old classroom door in a hallway after taking an elevator one up from the last entity room. The door has small wires in the glass and a steel door with tiny square wires for safety. They are met with a man who walks them down the hall to the door.

As we approach the door, another man stands inside the room and opens the door for us to walk in.

Agent Eph and Plateeney look at each other and step into the room. The man has this extended electronic device in his hand, similar to a cattle prod about three and a half feet long. It's a weird device, and we know it's just in case of an issue with the human entity. Still, it could be different for such a solid device to take down a person with such energy.

Agent Eph looks at the man with the prod and says, That's a little extreme?

The man says it's just for safety, but it's needed.

Agent Eph and Plateeney approach a couple of chairs in the middle of a classroom-type room.

Agent Eph: Well, at least we have the protection.

*There is a man in the center of the room, and he is staring at us both, and then he will view the guard and quickly back to Agent Eph. The chair the man is sitting in is a vintage desk with a chair and a covering like a fifties-style desk. It even has a small pencil sharpener on top, which we didn't expect to see in this room after the first interrogations. Yes, we both think it's weird, but we sit before this man and proceed. The desk on the floor is also chained, and his arms are on each side.

The man is clearly around thirty-five years of age and probably has a slight military background or possibly a parent who disciplined him while growing up because of his prim and proper appearance. He is wearing an oversized plaid shirt, tan and off-white with navy blue stripes. He wears glasses with stonewashed jeans and a short haircut like a crew cut. His shirt is also tucked in his pants, and he is wearing a brown-colored belt to match his brown and simple clothing but all together presentable like a shop teacher.

He looks like a decent guy except that the flannel shirt is very loud in appearance, and from the look on his face, you can tell he has been through life a bit from some early signs of wrinkling on the face. At thirty-five, you can see he was a smoker with a bit of weight in his stomach. But clearly, it's the shirt with the large blue and tan plaid. It just does not match; it's like he uses only half of his brain from memory on his dress and color choices. From intuition, we can tell that there may be activity other than himself as we approach him. Apparently, he is a guy you may want to keep a distance from before speaking to see his reaction. You would think he was more of a science teacher in your high school, especially choosing his desk.

His glasses are also vintage, with a black rim at only the top, similar to a style you would see in the late '50s, as a rectangle with thicker frames on the top and sides. The man does not look crazy like the channeled entity.

This guy looks normal, so he will probably be crazy, is what Plateeney is thinking.

Plateeney says, how are you? He approaches his body like he wants to shake hands, and the guard immediately moves his hand to say 'No.'

The human entity clearly does not like this.

The guard says: "No touching at all. It's OK if you have a problem with it."

The man makes a mean, scowl face and puts his head down like a child.

We are sitting about six feet from him, and the guard is in between us in front, but he is about two feet from the man as he is chained to the ground. It has something around his hands and wrists. That is clinching him to not move at all.

Agent Eph asks the man if he has a name.

He says his name is Harold. He says, Jenkins.

The guard looks at us to state that it's not his real name, but it's how he will be known today because he does not feel like himself. After all, we will not give him the decency to allow the conversation to begin with a handshake.

Agent Eph states, sorry they did not allow it; I would have shaken your hand.

Agent Eph raises her hand and says, How about a slight high five for the situation. He raises his head, looks at Agent Eph, and smiles.

It's almost like you understand now because of his face why there is the caution for there being no touching in the interrogation. He gives Agent Eph a look like he wants to eat her alive, and she slowly plays off the gesture and proceeds.

Plateeney looks at Harold, and his eyes roll back in his head. And he can sense that Harold may have an immediate sexual entity because he looks excited as if fantasizing about Agent Eph's touch.

Plateeney states I was, too, but I changed my mind.

Harold immediately made a weird half-face.

Plateeney slowly stands, and Harold clenches up as Plateeney pulls Agent Eph to the corner of the room and reminds her that we are not friends with this guy, so we may wanna stick to the interrogation mission because we have no idea what he is capable of this guy yet.

The two return to their seats, and Harold again puts his head down like a child.

Plateeney states, Do you enjoy thinking about women, Harry?

He says yes.

Plateeney continues: Do you wanna be here?

Harold shakes his head to say yes, stops, and does not say anything.

Plateeney: Can you explain why you are here?

Harold: I was forced to come here from the hospital, and they stated that I had some problems as I was brought here. I don't remember anything that happened. But they indicate that I did some things I don't remember and are trying to figure out why I don't.

Plateeney asks, What are they telling you that you did? He states that he was walking to his house in the middle of a regular suburban area. Apparently, someone was making fun of him in the front yard, and he doesn't remember anything after that. Apparently, this has happened for over a year. Many things have taken place, and he has just blacked out completely.

Plateeney: So basically, what you are telling me, Harry, is that you did something or some things, have no idea or no memories of them, but yet you are here?

Harold: Yes, that is the case. All I remember is certain things that people would do that anger me. Eventually, when I blacked out, I didn't remember anything else.

Plateeney asks: What did they tell you that you did?

Harold grows speechless and puts his head down again.

Plateeney says, What, Harold? We are here to learn about this situation.

Harold looks up and says that two younger kids around nineteen would always poke fun at me daily or every other day while walking on the sidewalk in front of my home. This was always on my walk home from school.

One day, one threw something at Harold, and he blacked out. The report states that he grabbed one of the kids by the arm, and when the kid tried to run away, he pulled him to the ground. He then jumped on top of him with his back to the ground. The other person saw this happen and tried to pull his friend, and Harold also pushed him to the ground. As he pushed the other kid to the ground, he apparently bit off a chunk out of the cheek area of his face. The other person saw this on the ground and ran away. When he began to run away. He jumped up, ran after him, caught him, and started biting him. Now, some other things took place, and a neighbor saw this and saw blood on the ground. Even though Harold does not remember anything, this person recognizes Harold and starts approaching him with an object.

Harold somehow took the object from him and used it on the neighbor trying to help, swung it, and struck this man on the side of the neck.

As the kids lay on the ground bleeding and moaning, he hit the neighbor again, pulling him nearer to the kids in his yard and hitting both children with it, killing them instantly. Harold then laid them on top of each other in the front yard. The kids were eighteen and twenty, and the neighbor was a parent and older. No one else saw this happen as Harold started the stacking and looked around. No one else was there, so Harold began to pull the bodies into his house so no one could see what he had done. Harold works quick and does this successfully. *And it says in the report that Harold commented that briefly, he does remember cleaning this situation up inside the home. But after this situation. He does not have a memory.

Before, Harold starts jumping over the fences away from the disaster he has created. After this, he jumps the fence and jumps the next fence. He cleans only briefly, so clearly, someone will find the bodies stacked in a home with a small blanket on top of them.

Now he goes home, still doesn't remember anything, and is calm, which seems strange. After a short time, he walks to a local bar, starts drinking, and remembers bits and pieces of what he thinks is a possible dream in his mindset.

So, as he is drinking, this is taking place, and he remembers more. He looks in his fingernails to see if he has a trace of blood. He does have some slight scratches on his hands from the altercation, and as he looks at his hands a little more, he vaguely starts to remember a tiny bit of what he did.

After this, he is on drink number four; someone walks in and starts a fight in the bar, and Harold gets aggravated. And he is close to finishing his drink and knows he wants another one. He gets slightly pushed in the middle of this fight, and you can tell he is unhappy.

Harold remains silent, and apparently, the guy who pushed the other one into him continues to speak with the man near the altercation. While this is brewing, the man sees Harold making faces and is unhappy with the words they are speaking to each other. He then starts to pick with Harold a bit, and as this occurs, Harold grabs a bottle, breaks it, and approaches the man who started taunting Harold.

As this gets greater, others immediately break the two up. Nothing happens after this. They cleaned the broken bottle like nothing and told the guy who started it with both men to leave and go home. Harold goes back to his seat and starts drinking again.

But now he has an alibi because the scratches on his hands could also be from the broken bottle at the bar.

One thing leads to another, and Harold gets really drunk that night at the bar. Someone is apparently trying to proposition him at the bar, and Harold is motivated.

This woman was a bartender at the bar, and Harold started to drunkenly get excited about this occurrence. The bartender was also under the influence pretty bad. Harold has a lot of built-up rage in him from the last 24 hours. He continues to step up the conversation sexually with the female bartender.

The stronger Harold draws closer to the female bartender, some people notice that he may be coming on too strong because the bartender starts to have a rougher conversation with Harold.

She walks from across the bar back behind the bar. Apparently, Harold is trying to make arrangements for a possible one-night stand.

The female bartender acts like she is interested but is more selective towards the whole approach and wants to get paid for any actions between them. Apparently, they go around back, and he turns into somebody completely different.

The police report states that she said he transformed into a completely different person. He does not remember a thing because he was entirely under alcohol.

She was under the influence of drugs and alcohol, which was later reported, and it also states that he forced sex on the bartender, which she states was forced. He does not remember a thing at all. The next thing you know, the report says she was poorly cut and slightly bruised on her legs.

Agent Eph: Was she raped?

There is no proof of it yet, but she is stating. Clearly, the police have a history of knowing she is on drugs and usually trying to solicit her body for sex, so they will allow the situation to be processed but are also taking things with caution due to the physical marks on the female.

You don't know what to think. The woman claimed that as they were about to get intimate, he turned into something like a fucking monster, she states during the situation.

Agent Eph: So basically, they were going to have sex, and then it got weird and rough.

Plateeney: She wanted money for sex, and I think he wanted to negotiate. As that continued, he drew angry and blacked out again. She started to get him horny. As she negotiated more and more for money, he continued to move forward with the process. But once again, no memory. She states the more it drew closer. Eventually, he threw her harder his way, she reports and continues. It is challenging for enforcement because he was insanely drunk. And she was drunk with a trace of drugs in her system.

Even better is the alibi with the fight, and then there is a murder in the town of three people in a home eight miles away. It is on the news and TV, and people have heard (the murders) have occurred, and it's quite a surprise. No one knows who it is or who or what.

Harold goes on his merry way, and slowly but surely, about six months go by. Minor altercations occur here and there. Some people around Harold may question if he has slight psychological issues. They call it mental issues, but realistically, the dude has some entity attachments from many levels of his psyche. This guy has had severe traumas in almost every aspect of his life. And every time he falls under the influence, one takes him over, and he blacks out a self-induced trauma.

He forgets everything and then moves on to the next occurrence.

Agent Eph: Clearly makes some sense, yes.

Plateeney: Harold clearly has a sexual entity, if not two. He has an alcohol entity. Harold is not on drugs but has an anger issue, so it would also be safe to state we know Harold has three entities present. But with the alcohol entity, that means every time he drinks, it's like another one on top of the other, which is an obsession with the build-up times seven. So there is an obsession entity within, too.

Agent Eph: What about the psychic?

Plateeney Clearly, Eph, this is not an issue. It might be, but we don't know his everyday life in this report. We were only given the whereabouts of what was learned from a folder. We are here to interrogate and investigate more to see through this learning experience. But apparently, it was a lousy case of entity issue. We can't take this guy's testimony for reality. Because he is talking and we are reading our folders, he clearly has no idea what the story is based on what we view in the briefing folders. But given the knowledge we know now about entities, we also know this literally happens in everyday human life or can.

We are given more than one example of the symptoms of life with entities and what to look out for before a disaster in your life. We are even seeing the pictures that he has done this, too. (to get a visual)

Agent Eph: So he is involved in all these things. Could he be a possible serial killer?

Plateeney: Well, I'm sure he can be a serial killer, but we only know what we have shown. I don't think there are any other murders in the town. There are still no murders in the city six months later, so he may not be a serial killer. Still, it could be the start of something in that direction, especially with the entities involved. We surely know it's the first stage of fucking entity possession. So, we have four of them, if not multiple others.

Agent Eph: The whisper and the channel could open it up slowly for the other five.

Plateeney: Yes, let's proceed. The psychic is the only one we really don't think is there. I believe he has more than one sexual entity and more than one alcohol. He can't control himself when it comes to drinking, so he has an obsession.

Agent Eph: Can you look at the file and see if he has a history of drugs?

Plateeney: I never read anything about drugs in his file, but we must remember that everyone in a real-life situation who comes in contact with Harold seems to be on drugs. So I am sure it's triggered somehow in others to get him a little bit on the blackout side or slightly more temperamental.

Agent Eph: Good point. Once they are on drugs, they know they can escalate their energy. So everything he comes in contact with is on drugs, so the drug entity is attached to him like an attraction. And then he looks halfway decent, so the drug entity immediately lingers and likes that for their habit. He does not seem like a straight-up scumbag. There are no severe warnings visually right away.

Plateeney: I have a question for Harry. Harry, is it OK if I call you Harry? Harry, what is your real name? My real name is Paul, but you see that in the folder. Yes, Paul, where are you from? Paul: New Hampshire.

Agent Eph: What is your last name? Richardson Paul Richardson from New Hampshire, what is your occupation or what used to be your occupation. I was a high school teacher. I taught political science.

Agent Eph: Did you have any affairs with female students as a teacher? Harold says No.

Agent Eph: OK, good.

Agent Eph: Any affairs with students, male or female. I never felt like I was a sexual celebrity they wanted to solicit in their minds. No, not at all to me.

Agent Eph: I am asking how would you ever pursue it? No, they would never either, so it was never a thought.

Agent Eph: So, political science, any other occupations before that? I used to be in the army for three years.

Agent Eph: You were discharged? Yes, for fighting

Agent Eph: Just fist-fighting? I had some problems with an officer.

Agent Eph: What happened, basically? He was picking on me quite a bit, and I couldn't handle it.

Agent Eph: You lost your temper and just lost it. I am trying to remember what happened. Yes, that's what they tell me.

Agent Eph: Have you ever been married to any kids? I don't have any children; I was almost married once.

Agent Eph: What happened with the relationship?

We were together for some time, she, I don't know; I caught her cheating. I came home one day, and she was cheating.

Agent Eph: That must have been devastating.

Harold: It's the one time I can say I didn't get mad.

Agent Eph: Has this ever happened to you before? No, not that I know if I still can't believe that I just watched it while it was happening, and after, I mean, I just walked out.

Agent Eph: When did you start feeling obsessed with the sexual entity? I am not aware of what you are talking about.

Agent Eph: OK, did you ever have a high sex drive or active life that was out of control.

Paul: No.

Agent Eph: Just normal?

Paul: I don't even know what normal would be, but I guess I'm trying to understand. I suppose you know the only time I ever think about anything sexual is drinking.

Agent Eph: Do you blackout when you drink?

Paul: It could happen more than expected, but after I drink for a while, I don't drive, so I don't really have a meter that tells me to stop, so I don't feel it's a problem.

Agent Eph: Have you ever woken up next to a female you didn't know?

Paul: No.

Agent Eph: I am trying to understand when the sexual entity became a role in your life?

Paul: Well, I don't understand sexual entity at all.

Agent Eph: Well, it would be a force convincing you that you need to have the urge to have sex; a lot may be unhealthy.

Paul: Do you have sex?

Agent Eph: I will not answer any personal questions from you. This is just a Q and A from me to you but for you.

Paul: OK.

Agent Eph: This is just an interview for you.

Paul: OK.

Plateeney, we must go along with Agent Eph if needed.

Paul: I have no idea what a sexual entity is.

Agent Eph: I tried to explain, but I don't think you listen.

Paul: It was too difficult. I was thinking about you.

Agent Eph looks at Plateeney and says, oh God.

Agent Eph: I will ask my partner to explain it to you. (with brief anger)

Plateeney: OK, Harry, clearly you have a little bit of a crush on Agent Eph. Do you know why you would have a crush on Agent Eph?

Paul: I don't have a crush on Agent Eph.

Plateeney: OK. Well, why would you ask Agent Eph if she had sex?

Paul: I think about what she would do if she did.

Plateeney: Which makes sense? How?

Paul: I don't know. I reflect on the aspect of why.

Plateeney: OK, thank you. I have another question. How often would you say you had sex in a month?

Paul: Probably about twice a month, that I remember.

Plateeney: How much do you drink when you go to a bar? I'll ask three questions. Do you drink at a bar? Do you drink at private functions? Do you drink at home?

Paul: I don't drink at home. I don't have alcohol at home; many people don't even know I drink.

Plateeney: How often do you go to a bar?

Paul: I go to a bar probably three times a week. Plateeney: Is that where you meet people to have sex twice a month?

Paul: Yes... but it's never people I date. People are always trying to get me into a situation, and they will eventually ask for money somehow?

Plateeney: So, a prostitute?

Paul: Not really a prostitute.

Agent Eph: Escorts?

Paul: I don't know what you would call them, but they start talking to you and don't even ask you to buy them a drink. Next thing you know, they get to know me better, and I get a little more relaxed. Then they say, "Hey, if you give me a hundred dollars, I'll give you a blow job."

Agent Eph: OK.

Paul: It's always something like that. That's what you experience at some of these places.

Plateeney: What are they? Bars or strip clubs? Paul: It's more like just a regular bar.

Plateeney: OK, I am starting to understand. Do you have any hobbies?

Paul: No, the only thing I did other than go to a bar and work was cut my grass, that's it.

Plateeney says, Excuse us for a moment. The two take a step into the hall for a brief moment.

Plateeney explains to Agent Eph: This will get graphic, Eph, so prepare for it. He cannot focus on me at all. He is still focusing on you, and he gets a little fidgety. He is looking at you, basically. What is happening to him is strange.

Agent Eph: Is something taking him over? Like an entity?

Plateeney: The alcohol entity can't intervene because he is clearly not drinking. The obsession entity is there, but he can't get out of his mind that he wants to have sex with you, so you must be as creative as possible. Please do not allow the entity's gestures to make you mad, Agent Eph. We are trying to see what is happening with him mentally. We can help others from possibly being in the same situation.

Agent Eph: OK, I get it. Don't like it, but I understand.

Plateeney: I will drive the sexual entity to come out so you can question the sexual entity within the human. We must remember that this guy killed three people and possibly raped somebody he almost killed. He doesn't fucking know he did it? He can't move...he will try to, but he can't. He may even try to come at you.

Agent Eph: Right... do we feel like his other personality that he blocked out and is taking over is getting out? And yes, I will be ready. Thank you for the description; it helps a lot.

Plateeney: Yes, and I will bring out the entity when it happens. You start to question it so we can learn, and I will ask the entity questions, but he will never look at me. He is going to stare at you the whole time.

Agent Eph: Do I need to chime in or listen?

Plateeney: You must ask the entity questions because he is interested in you.

Agent Eph: OK. Got it. As the pair walked back into the room, Harry convulsed a bit. His legs are first, and he puts his arms up on the desk and acts like he doesn't want to talk to me anymore. (Plateeney) He barely speaks as he says I don't want to talk to you anymore. He is telling Plateeney this, and he starts shaking his head, and he is now the sexual entity. You can clearly observe something wrong with him when he does this. It's clearly some Heckle and Jeckyl strangeness. Now he tries to stand up on the desk, and as he does this, it's like he wants to come towards you, and you freak out a bit with a strange face. As he reaches towards a bit, you get out of your chair and step back. He says I'm sorry, and then he comes at you because Harry knows he startled you, but he can't move forward because the chains stop him.

We need to talk about this while it's in him because he is not Paul anymore. He has become the sexual entity for sure at this point. Still, He keeps in mind that we will discuss the sexual entity and the obsession.

But remember, it may be hard to differentiate between the two. OK, so the obsession and the sexual entity will talk to you.

Agent Eph: Perfect, got it.

Plateeney: It's hard to describe to others because you have to describe what it's doing and thinking. Your composure is most important because it's you that it wants to feed on. But you know clearly, Harold can't do anything. I want you to understand that I don't want you to go through trauma during this interrogation.

At this point, he is actually standing up and pulling on the chains like a hungry entity zombie. He would like to break these chains. Now he is looking at us both, and at you saying, I am sorry with his hands in front of him. I'm sorry. I didn't mean to scare you. He is saying I didn't mean to scare you. He is actually trying to manipulate you at this time.

Agent Eph: OK, you didn't mean to scare me. Paul, I don't know how to explain that. I didn't mean to scare you. You don't need to stand up. What is going through your mind right now?

Paul: I want you to sit down.

Agent Eph: OK, I am sitting down. Let's talk.

Paul: OK.

Agent Eph: My partner is just going to observe. We are just going to talk.

Plateeney: Are you, Harry, right now?

Paul: No, I'm not Harry!

Agent Eph: You're not?

Paul: Not at all.

Agent Eph: You someone else?

Paul: Yes, I am.

Agent Eph: OK. Alright.

Paul: Harry has no idea who I am at this point.

Agent Eph: No idea.

Paul: Yes.

Agent Eph: Do you have a name for it?

Paul: Not at all. I don't need one.

Agent Eph: What is going on with you right now?

Paul: "I want you, Eph." Agent Eph: What does that mean?

Paul: I want you. (says slowly) If my body could not be contained now, I would be on top of you for some reason.

Agent Eph: Attacking me?

Paul: No, you turn me on.

Agent Eph: OK, how do I turn you on.

Paul: Your hair, Eph.

Agent Eph: OK, so you get turned on by my hair? Long hair or short hair?

Paul: It does not matter.

Agent Eph: OK. Well, that's all I need to know she chuckles a bit.

Plateeney: How were you able to take Harry over? Is what you need to be asking?

Agent Eph: How did you come out of Paul's consciousness? What was the trigger?

Paul: Harry does not want to be a person that thinks sexually. He has allowed me to take that part of his mind over.

Agent Eph: OK.

Paul: Harry has an average sexual life based on what he explained.

Paul: He does not have a clue what he has done. That is my job.

Agent Eph: OK. So how did you, and can you use him as a host because he seems like a nice guy without your help. How did you take him over?

Paul: I didn't do anything. He wanted it to happen.

Agent Eph: He wanted it?

Paul: Harry became quite obsessed with the situation with his ex as he watched her have sex with someone else. It traumatized him as he watched.

Agent Eph: I would have slammed the door. So, was he turned on by this visual?

Paul: I was, and that's when I was starting to take over.

Agent Eph: And that's why he stayed, as he was traumatized?

Paul: Yes. As he was traumatized.

Agent Eph: So you took advantage of his vulnerability at that point.

Paul: Absolutely.

Agent Eph: You started with the whisper and gave him sexual fantasies.

Paul: How do you know what the whisper is?

Agent Eph: I have already talked to the whisper.

Paul: OK, that turns me on even more.

Agent Eph: (Makes a face) and says So you started after the messages from the whisper released her messages.

Paul: The Whisperer's message was just one word: "Failure." The more he thought he was a failure, the more we almost had total control. We are almost at the point where we have all of him.

Agent Eph: So he was butchered emotionally and mentally. You continued to hammer him with little confidence and low power, but he has a military background.

Paul: That's what they told him, too.

Agent Eph: They beat him down, and he never was built back up or restored his confidence. He felt unmanly.

Paul: When you break a person down, you build them back up to who you are trying to program that person to be. He was never built back up and programmed.

Agent Eph: Did they do that on purpose, or did it just happen that way.

Paul: It's part of the process. That's why we immediately try to go after those types of men and women. We are not prejudiced.

Agent Eph: So he never had a positive upbringing of confidence.

Paul: He had confidence when he was young. But he always had anger problems. He slowly became obsessed. He was at a point where he began to believe that he was a failure at thirteen. Then the whisper and the channeler were there, and we took over and left. We could come back as he slowly conquered what we were doing shortly after his military experience. Then, he slowly attracted certain people into his life to feed more and more. Many of the people we attract also have entities too. They all just were not aware of it. They were all disguised until we were ready to implement our feeding procedures.

Agent Eph: Would he be a horrible case of overactive, driven entities?

Paul: He is not bad at all.

Agent Eph: But he is chained.

Paul: He is only chained up because he got caught.

Agent Eph: So there are many of these running around and possibly worse?

Paul: Yes, I would say so.

Agent Eph: So, should we go back to questioning Harry?

Paul: The only reason I am talking to you now is that I can't stop thinking about you. You know, much like an obsession.

Agent Eph: So you are the entity.

Paul: Yes.

Agent Eph: I have some questions for Harry.

Paul: He is not here.

Agent Eph: What is your sexual thing? Is it an issue with women what it is?

Paul: It could be just looking at a woman.

Agent Eph: OK, is it all women?

Paul: The majority. It just depends on what I can get my host to do. I can feel better with oppressed women with similar problems if he has anger issues. Problems with men that have beaten them or issues that have occurred negatively.

Agent Eph: Are there any things he is not attracted to. He is not attracted to children, which we are not always happy about because a child's fear has an energy we enjoy quite a bit.

Agent Eph: You are pathetic. Fucking pathetic.

Paul: Thank you.

Agent Eph: I will get through this interview.

Plateeney: I have a question for the obsession entity. How did you get in there before the sexual entity?

Paul: How do you know there is another entity. (angry)

Plateeney: Because for him to be obsessed with the fact that he gave up his sexuality, he had to become obsessed with it, and he was apparently obsessed with anger. So the excitement drew him to be obsessed, and obviously, it has drawn him to the point where he allowed that part of him to be taken over. So why don't you tell me how the obsession entity was able to jump in there before the sexual entity was able to step in?

Paul: We don't like each other. I am taking over.

Plateeney: You say you want to take full credit for this takeover.

Paul: That is right. It's all me. It's my takeover.

Plateeney: Even though you know the obsession got there before. You won't admit that it did.

Paul: No, I won't. It's all me. It's mine.

Plateeney: Can you take a break or step back to speak to the obsession entity, as I ask? Paul: Fine.

Paul: (obsession entity) His anger made him obsessed to the point that he didn't care about who he was or allowed his soul to completely disconnect. Whenever his soul divided, we could fulfill the parts of his mind and body he didn't care about anymore. So we filled it with obsession. And after the obsession, the entity could take over every single day. We would always work the area he was angry about to the point that if he was mad about something or stubbed his toe, we made sure he kept thinking about it all day. He constantly kept thinking about stubbing his toe all day like an obsession. He consistently kept thinking about his issue.

We ensured something else fueled the fire until anger took over like an explosion. The more Harold grew angry, he would forget who he was, and we knew that was our way in. It's a lot like hacking a computer program. If you see a hole, you try to figure out how to get in, attaching to that situation. It's not the person that we are trying to hurt. You were getting mad a second ago about him bringing up children. He's just trying to drive sexuality about to make the host forget. It's not the fact that you are angry. It's the overall fact that you stay angry. (possibly those around him, too) It shows that he can manipulate you similarly, and they feed off that situation. He is showing that you can also be taken over the same way. They enjoy seeing that they are in control, which opens you up to their control.

Agent Eph: I am defending something, but I hear you saying.

Paul: (obsession entity): You must understand that this entity can care less about anything you care about. They are programmed to make you hate and feel anger because they feed off them. It's no different than you getting excited to eat your favorite food. The only difference is that they know how to make you use your emotions to allow them to disconnect you from your soul even more. They don't care. This thing does not even want me to be here, and I am why he was allowed to enter this host. Eventually, the more robust and controlled it gets, the more it will not allow me to speak when spoken to. It's a human with too much egotism. He was pissed the second I was even brought up. Once the sexual entity is there, it will be an act of God before it goes. So that aspect of who you are better not be high because it will never leave. It is not getting better, either. It's similar to a human addiction to a cigarette.

They never forget. When a human smokes a cigarette, it's pretty addictive and allows us to read how much it takes over. It's an excellent substance for an entity because it will become angry when not smoking. It's worst that they may quit, but many always want to smoke. The more memories we put there, it's better for us. The more solitary you bring them in, the more they think about it because the entity can make them forget who they are. They will become the entity fully in prison. They are smart enough to make you think that they don't think. That's how intelligent the thing is. Whatever it has to do to feed is what it will do, even to the extent of feeding off another host near it. Yes, eating another person or taking a bite to scare someone in the room is extreme, but if the entity feels he can get a rise off something or someone, it will do that. If the entity can make another person feel fearful in a sexual way, it will do it. This is its favorite, by the way. If it's a child, it does not matter what it is, even a fucking animal. An animal can see into the etheric dimension and have a high fear factor. It can view what is happening without emotion because there is no life, but it does indeed feel. This is what you have to understand. It's not a personal thing. This is what they are programmed to do. I'm sharing this because your job is so important because of your responsibility for learning when you are out and about. It would help if you controlled your mind and emotions because the entity would drive you to anger. After all, it knows that that is the easiest way to take you over and make yourself stronger. You have to contain your anger even in the worst situations.

Agent Eph: We have to try and defend ourselves in some situations.

Paul (obsession entity): You can protect yourself when they try to attack you. If they try to attack, you kill them because we die. Unless, for some reason, we can escape the host before the life force energy leaves the body. But one of us is going to die. The chances of it being the one that is selfish first are that the sexual entity will try to survive before anything else.

Agent Eph: Do I need to continue interviewing the sexual entity? Do we still have more to cover?

Paul (obsession entity): A little.

Agent Eph: So I asked you if there is any other female they are not attracted to besides what we just talked about?

Paul (obsession entity): No. It's an obsession. They don't care what it is as long as they can feel sexual energy or fear from another person; that's what they want. It's not the fact that it turns them on sexually. It's the "want" to feel fear and anger because that anger fuels an element of energy. It's not the fact that it's a sexual thing. I think that's where you can't understand. The host has allowed him or herself to be completely taken over. It's almost like you think of the brain as six different color sections. It will say, OK, this part is mine now. So when you put a thought near this section, the particular entity states electronically. OK, this is mine now. It believes that it owns your thoughts at that point because somewhere along the line, it has manipulated you to the point that you consciously and subconsciously said it was OK. Whenever it goes near happiness, if that entity controls that aspect of the brain or you told it, it can. This is why dealing with trauma is so traumatic. Because the host allowed the entity to move forward because it was too mentally challenging to deal with the thought. Not knowing what it will do to his life. Harry will be locked up for fifty years.

Agent Eph: Are you the obsession entity?

Paul (obsession entity): Yes.

Agent Eph: We will go back to.

Paul (obsession entity): Here's the deal I win in prison. I am still obsessed with prison, no matter what it is. If he continues to fulfill his sexual needs in prison, he will win. But if not, if he is solitary, I am still obsessed, and it will keep driving him. I will eventually win unless his other entities get to where he feels it's time to vacate the premises for someone else. He can be on top and then move to another person. So we go back and forth. This is why we don't like sharing entities. It never ends between us. You have to understand that we are both here to survive, and it's almost like I am a little guy, and he's pushing me to climb a wall. He is coming back now, by the way.

Agent Eph: OK. Is there something that I need to know that any information would help us with your entity?

Paul (sexual entity): I don't want to speak to you; I think about you.

Agent Eph: OK, alright, what are those thoughts, Paul, and what is it about the energy you like?

Paul: You hate me. It's very fascinating to me.

Agent Eph: I don't hate you. I have no emotion for you.

Paul: That's even better for me.

Agent Eph: Well, it does not matter to me either way.

Paul: You are such a liar.

Agent Eph: I'm here to learn more about you and complete a task. Let's talk.

Paul: If you were here to get a job done, you failed the test.

Agent Eph: How did I fail the test?

Paul: Your job is to make me happy.

Agent Eph: My job is to get information from you. You are instructed to follow protocol, so it's time to comply with some of the instructions you were given before you even walked into this room today.

Paul: Oh no, I'm not instructed by him. I control your friend here, who has no idea he is being played like a robot. Agent Eph: You are in control of Paul but not the situation. Paul: I'm more in control than you think.

Agent Eph: Well, that is your illusion.

Paul: As long as you keep talking to me like that, I am perfectly OK.

Agent Eph: OK, maybe we will get somewhere. Is there any helpful information you want to give me about the sexual entity?

Paul: Can you repeat sex?

Agent Eph: The sex...sexual entity.

Paul: You said it twice, thank you. You remind me of that prostitute speaking like that.

Agent Eph: What is something we don't know a sexual entity might do. Something we are not aware of.

Paul: Right now, I am just thinking about you.

Agent Eph: What exactly would it take to get you to answer these questions?

Plateeney: I am going to stop you both for a second. (walks away with Agent Eph briefly) "You are being tested." You are too angry to understand what you are being tested to see, But that is what's happening. What is the one thing you would do to fight something terrible?

Agent Eph: I would be in control.

Plateeney: It has nothing to do with control. Control is what is feeding that thing.

Agent Eph: Control of my emotions.

Plateeney: You have to completely control your emotions right now. How do you fight negativity?

Agent Eph: With negativity.

Plateeney: How do you fight hate?

Agent Eph: With love.

Plateeney: Thank you.

Agent Eph: But that thing does not understand love.

Plateeney: It does not matter. It still has hate. It's feeding off your anger and subconscious because you don't create sacred space. The subconscious can be manipulated because there is no sacred space before the interview. It's a test. You have to do it in the middle of the talk to tell me what you are doing. We are going to go back to that scenario. You have to create a sacred space in the middle of it. OK, here we go.

Agent Eph: OK, Paul, whoever has taken over Harry or Paul, you ready to talk again?

Paul: I will think about you a little more, much deeper this time. I'm just going to enjoy every bit of it.

Agent Eph: Go right ahead. I'm going to create some sacred space right now.

Plateeney: You don't need to tell him that. You know we are not in a church, Eph.

Agent Eph: Starts laughing.

Plateeney: The energy of your thoughts will create it, Eph. The layer between you and him. Yes, I feel it. You cannot improvise, but congratulations, you finally created a sacred space.

Paul: Have you ever fantasized about wild and crazy stuff?

Agent Eph: Who am I talking to right now?

Paul: Who do you think? Agent Eph: Have I ever done that? No... I mean, yeah, I have.

Paul: Oh, this is awesome. Tell me.

Agent Eph: You know my memory is not OK.

Plateeney: (breathes heavily and gestures to Eph) Seriously, Eph, how will you converse about sex with the sexual entity? I think this will help us in our interrogation. We are being tested.

Agent Eph: Don't get mad, OK... alright.

Plateeney: We don't need information. We have already interrogated the entity from before. We are here to fight the entity.

Agent Eph: Don't get mad.

Plateeney: Listen to this. Read back. I feed off of sex and sexual thoughts, and now we are talking about your fantasies. It just makes him want to keep asking the same circular questions repeatedly.

Agent Eph: OK, I get it. I am feeding it with the answering of the questions.

Plateeney: What are you an agent for? Tell me your deepest sexual fantasies, Agent Eph...

Agent Eph: Fuck No!

Plateeney: When you say "Fuck" you know what that does to this thing? It makes it power up and want more.

Agent Eph: OK, I'm not going to do that.

Paul: Tell me more about your fantasies...

Agent Eph: I am here to ask questions and not answer them.

Paul: But you said you had some deep sexual fantasies. I want to feel them.

Agent Eph: You can feel what you like.

Paul: This makes me even crazier.

Agent Eph: I'm good here. I don't have any more questions. Thank you.

Paul: What are you doing? Are you mad?

Agent Eph: I am great. I'm just relaxing.

Paul: You are doing something else.

Agent Eph: No, I'm just sitting down. Not just sitting down.

Agent Eph: I will wrap this up, and thank you.

Paul: Thank you.

Plateeney: What are you doing?

Agent Eph: I wrapped this up, so I will no longer ask any more questions.

Paul: How were you able to do that. Listen to me.

Agent Eph: Can someone explain to Paul that I am no longer answering questions?

Paul: How were you able to block me? That's not what you did. You were able to block my energy from the feeling of your fantasies. How were you able to do that.

Agent Eph: I stopped feeding on your energy of anger, and I didn't give you the feeling of anger anymore.

Paul: What did you give me?

Agent Eph: I gave you peace, so I didn't open up opportunities to get in, but you were trying hard.

Paul: The word hard is pretty awesome. Agent Eph: Well, you have a great day.

Paul: You too.

Plateeney: Harry, are you back? Paul: Yeah, I am. What happened?

Agent Eph: We had an interview, but it wasn't you. It was something that took over you. We believe that there are five of them, possibly seven. This particular one is called the sexual entity, which has taken over your life and is not even close to your actual personality. Harry or Paul has no exciting sexual life or activity, and this son of a bitch is freaking a horny toad. He has raped a few women. Basically, anything with two legs and a female is all over.

Paul: So you are telling me that I?

Agent Eph: Yes, you have raped women, attacked women, you actually tried to attack me and try to overcome me.

Paul: Why do I not remember any of this at all?

Agent Eph: Because he completely takes over your personality.

Plateeney: But clearly, he states that you allowed him to take you over. It's your free will in jeopardy, apparently. Some of you allowed him to take you over, and you must understand that even though you don't remember, it's still you because your permission was granted. You could not handle anger from the past or a past situation. This part of your brain and central nervous system controls the aspects of sexuality that mess with you till you don't care anymore. Once you no longer care, you allow these things to be taken over, so you don't have to think about it. It's not different than taking a drug, so you don't have to think about the pain. There are entities in that, too. It's just that you have never done drugs to know. You started with obsession, and then it became stronger with the sexual entity.

Once you didn't care about the sexuality of who you were, you allowed other things to take you over. In that aspect, once your energy becomes more vital, this thing would take that part of you over, and you would become something else. It was always triggered by alcohol. It's now at the point that the sexual entity can ultimately take you over because you don't want to think about you doing something wrong.

Paul: So you are telling me I killed three people, almost killed another person, and almost tried to do something to Agent Eph?

Agent Eph: Yes.

Paul: So what will happen to me?

Agent Eph: Right now, you are chained up... What will happen to you? You will not return to society unless there is some way to eradicate these entities.

Paul: How do you remove something you can't even see?

Agent Eph: The way I understand it is there is a way to do it.

Paul: There may be a way to do it, but they need help.

Agent Eph: Until then, you are stuck here, unfortunately. But as long as you have these entities, there is no way you can be around anyone.

Paul: So what happened?

Agent Eph: You are stuck in this situation. It's like a prison; you have a guard, and anyone or anything you come in contact with will have to be chained up because they have entirely controlled you.

Paul: I mean, I would rather not be here in my own mind. If this is something that I did, I remember wanting to think about only a few of these things. I remember coming on several different occasions where someone was next to me. You know I wasn't happy and possibly scared. I didn't even know what was going on. The situation was over, and I felt like I needed to leave. But it's not me.

Agent Eph: We know it's not you because of the sudden personality changes. I would have liked to ask about the sexual entity because we know many different levels of sexual entity attachment. I am unsure how to describe it, but I wondered how many you had.

Paul: I don't know. This is definitely the first time anyone has asked me anything like this.

Agent Eph: We are aware of a solid sexual entity present. We know that there is no urge toward children. That wasn't the issue. But they said they tried. There were no same-sex attractions as well.

It seems to get into prostitutes, and we know of some rape and abuse, so it's rough. It's very slick-talking. It takes advantage of vulnerable, weak women. It's really slick and pushes your buttons. There is very smooth talking involved, for sure.

Paul: So how did it try to get something from you?

Agent Eph: It tried to piss me off. I felt myself getting rattled. Different space and different all-around energy. I decided to get calm and not allow it to make me angry. And then I just ended it.

Paul: And that was it. It looks like a school, but it's more like a strange prison. So, where do I go next? Where am I?

Agent Eph: I don't have the answers. We have yet to get to that point.

Paul: I don't know if I can. I mean, what do you research.

Agent Eph: You must go within and shield yourself because you have been mainly exposed. You are fine as long as you are Paul, but it's similar to a Ware-wolf transformation when they start taking over. It's like you become something else. When the full moon comes out, it's like hell.

Paul: OK. So what happens if I kill myself?

Agent Eph: Your next soul will be full of entities because you have not dealt with them in this life. That is what my intuition guides me to share with you now.

Plateeney: Harry, when is the last time you remember praying?

Paul: I don't remember doing that in a long time.

Plateeney: That is probably a start in the right direction. You can't think about where you are going. You have to think about what you're going to do, and giving up will not be a solution that will bring anybody's life back that you will take. If you take your life, you will come back just as fast because your choice to come here was yours. Your choice to allow something to take you over was your choice, too. The answer is not to give up. The answer is to keep everything from taking you over. It's a test for every single person on this planet. The test is basically to find whatever it is. The state of mind allows you to move forward, so you must return to when anger was your biggest problem. The entity told us that anger was our biggest problem. That's how it could take you over slowly, but you allowed it to take you over because of your anger. Slowly but steadily, the anger you portrayed on other people made you obsessed with anger and took it out on others.

Once the obsession took over, the sexual parts took over when you could not take over anymore. So when love was able to distance itself from you, you disconnected yourself from your soul. You allowed these things to take you over when you disconnected yourself from your soul. At that point, you chose to do that because you had free will and allowed it to be taken over by these entities. So, if you want your free will back, you must find a way to find love again. You need to figure out how to conquer and release whatever anger you have dealt with. You have to remember something. Taking another person's life and different situations you have done... will set up a certain amount of karmic energy. You may not actually deal with this life you are currently in. You may have to deal with it in the next four. But you will deal with it.

And if you choose to move on and hurt more, you will deal with it later. You may even be put somewhere else. Currently, it's still your choice. It's still your choice. Whether or not you did something good or terrible, it's your choice to move forward. It's also your choice to stop, but it's still your choice.

Whenever your soul moves on from its body, it will still hold on to those energies. It will be released once you discover how and why you can release them. If you have not dealt with these things, you will find yourself again when you return.

Agent Eph: Yep, that makes sense. Does that help Paul?

Paul: It helps me to understand how it happened. I don't remember feeling love in years. I don't remember feeling like I even cared to have sex with anything in a long time. Apparently, the anger was the drinking. The anger brought it out. I know that's what it is because every time I drank, it was the drinking it always started with. Then, something sexual after that. Drinking was my obsession because drinking was what I wanted every day when I would get tired or aggravated.

Agent Eph: Can we go back in your mind, maybe when you were a child, and you actually remember love? Tell me when you get there?

Paul: The last time I remember what love would feel like was playing baseball when I was a child.

Agent Eph: How old were you?

Paul: I had to be around seven.

Agent Eph: Go back to a time and visualize what it was like, the field, the people you were around, maybe what was the position that you played?

Paul: I really didn't play a position. I was more outfield. It was just hitting the ball.

Agent Eph: Were you good?

Paul: I don't remember, but I remember feeling good about being a kid. Not to feel anything. Carefree. That part of me didn't care.

Agent Eph: You were out there and carefree

Paul: Being a kid and releasing everything was great, but it felt good not to have to take care of anything. It's also my worst enemy because the more I didn't care, the more the entities took me over. What happened was love turned into hate. Not caring is what got me into this mess. When I think about that, it makes me think about better childhood memories. Being lonely, you don't think about what could happen to you.

Agent Eph: Did you have a happy childhood? How were your mom and dad? Did you have brothers and sisters?

Paul: Yeah, Mom and Dad were OK. I had an everyday life. I also had brothers and a sister. Yes.

Agent Eph: Did you get along with them?

Paul: As much as a kid could. Nothing abnormal, though, for sure. I wonder if they have these issues now that you say it.

Agent Eph: So you had a pretty healthy upbringing.

Paul: Yeah. Agent Eph: Were your parents affectionate? Do you remember hugs and possible praise as a child? Have you ever had any memories of your parents or family saying they loved or were proud of you?

Paul: I mean, I remember coaches telling you good job, and parents were expected, but every time I would cry, my dad would tell me you need to cry somewhere else. That's not something you need to do in front of me.

Agent Eph: That could be typical. Yeah, but it could create an issue as well. So, you never had a soft place to land with your emotions when upset?

Paul: I guess so. You know, I mean, everything else just happened. It was something I should have talked about. It was always something that just happened.

Agent Eph: I wonder if there was ever a place of pure, defined love?

Paul: I don't think I have ever felt that.

Agent Eph: OK. Even from a girlfriend or anybody, a teacher?

Paul: No.

Agent Eph: How do you feel, love?

Paul: I don't know. As I said, I could only think of what that meant when I hit a baseball with a bat.

Agent Eph: I am trying to help you get to that point, and if you have a memory of where you can go, I will try to get there.

Paul: I'm just telling you what I know.

Plateeney: Harry, I hear you don't know what love is.

Paul: That's precisely what I'm saying.

Plateeney: How do you figure out how to get that back. What it is that I am hearing is that you have given up the ability to love, and that is how these entities have taken you over to the point where you cannot love yourself. It's an inspiration to know what that feels like.

Agent Eph: Yeah, and, interestingly, he never had that love experience in his lifetime.

Plateeney: It's not that he didn't have it, more like he didn't know what the hell it was, and every time he tried to experience it, someone told him it wasn't manly or something like that. It's one of those situations where you are experiencing something psychologically wrong for you if you can't find something to love.

Agent Eph: It's a block, a total block.

Plateeney: Yeah, it creates a block.

Agent Eph: I can return to my earliest childhood memories and remember a feeling of love.

Plateeney: Yeah, but even his earliest memory of love is hitting something.

Agent Eph: Interestingly, this was his love experience.

Paul: But it's physical aggression. Like hitting a baseball or punching a punching bag, being let out is just love because or feeling a release.

Agent Eph: Was it kind of peace?

Paul: It's the only time I can think of what that would mean.

Agent Eph: When you talk to people, do you love people?

Paul: I remember always wanting to shake a person's hand, and they always wanted to hug me, which scared me.

Agent Eph: So you are not comfortable with affection.

Paul: It's not that. I'm uncomfortable with it; they want to give me love, but I am somehow scared of that feeling.

Agent Eph: I understand. Besides that fact, I know some people are not comfortable with hugging. How about just meeting someone really nice and pleasant. Do you have any emotions towards those people like this person charming? I wish somebody a positive thought.

Paul: I don't know.

Agent Eph: It's about time to wrap it up, but I want you to know that I am rooting for you, and I feel that when the entities are not around, you are a terrific guy. It's a shame that these entities were able to attach themselves to you. And I would encourage you to dig deep and fight like hell and get them suckers off you. Get them removed so you can escape this hell hole.

Paul: I wish somebody would tell me that I had this. I had no idea this even existed.

Agent Eph: We are just doing this particular project. If we would not do this, you may have never known.

Paul: It makes sense to take my mind over because it's so easy. I mean, no one has ever told me this. My parents certainly couldn't educate me on such a thing.

Agent Eph: They probably didn't know.

Paul: You only hear that the devil will get you. So you grow up thinking the devil will get me...but you never see a devil. You know, it's always some shady character in the background. That's how it's written about and everything. And you know the sad part about it is that.... the devil is me.

Agent Eph: That is a sad story, and it's not you. It's just something that took over you.

Paul: It's something I allowed to take over me.

Agent Eph: Consciously not even knowing.

Paul: It's a metaphor for life.

Agent Eph: It could teach others you were such a young kid when this started that as you got older, I can't say you did anything an average person would have done. You have done everything correctly.

Paul: I killed three people.

Agent Eph: You did kill three people, but your behavior as Paul, you know it's the entities, really.

Paul: But it's still me, and that's what I am saying. The devil is me... It's really me because it's the entity that chooses the entity. After all, the human allows it to be the host for a reason. I allowed that reason. You know all these things that they make you believe. It's fear. The whole fact that fear exists is the entity. So it's you now.

Plateeney: Harry, I specifically came here because I wanted to bring back the people's knowledge. The things that they were being lied to. I specifically came back to this time because, in the future, there will be more than 50,000 Harry's out there. So, if it makes you feel any better when we journal this, it will be the first time it's ever documented.

So other people will understand what you're dealing with, what you're going through, and what you are trying to figure out right now. You're dealing with thoughts of not being here anymore. We tell you that you will still have to deal with those issues. No one has ever heard anything like that. No one has had to rehabilitate themselves in that way. I am telling you that the vision of the future is the same way. Animals are put to sleep because they are in a place for too long, and no one can care for them. The same thing will happen to humans in the future if they do not understand that they can be taken over. So, if it makes you feel any better about whatever you're dealing with. Because you can't feel what love really is, understand that what you're dealing with will help other people.

Agent Eph: Yes, absolutely.

Plateeney: We will end it here, and the end of it will be that Harry smiled. That's it.

Agent Eph and Plateeney stand up, look at the guard, nod to Harry, and then start walking down the hall. As they walk down the hallway, Agent Eph and Plateeney know their training may have been strange. Still, as they walk down the corridor, they make eye contact, and Plateeney smiles at Agent Eph and says aloud.

"It's certainly not Cinderella."

"Somehow, you need to find yourself where it all started and deal with these traumas and issues so you can evict the problems inside of yourself." ~ The Entity Phylum.

Printed in the United States
by Baker & Taylor Publisher Services